CENTRIFUGE

Hilary Green

Chivers Press • Thorndike Press
Bath, England   Waterville, Maine USA

This Large Print edition is published by Chivers Press, England, and by Thorndike Press, USA.

Published in 2003 in the U.K. by arrangement with the author.

Published in 2003 in the U.S. by arrangement with Hilary Green.

U.K. Hardcover   ISBN 0–7540–8936–3 (Chivers Large Print)
U.K. Softcover   ISBN 0–7540–8937–1 (Camden Large Print)
U.S. Softcover   ISBN 0–7862–5141–7 (Nightingale Series)

The 6 lines from "The Second Coming" by W. B. Yeats are quoted by permission of M. B. Yeats, Miss Anne Yeats and the Macmillan Co. of London and Basingstoke.

The text of this Large Print edition is unabridged.
Other aspects of the book may vary from the original edition.

Set in 16 pt. New Times Roman.

Printed in Great Britain on acid-free paper.

British Library Cataloguing in Publication Data available

Library of Congress Cataloging-in-Publication Data

Green, Hilary, 1937–
    Centrifuge / by Hilary Green.
      p.   cm.
    ISBN 0–7862–5141–7 (lg. print : sc : alk. paper)
    1. Political violence—Fiction. 2. England—Fiction. 3. Large type books. I. Title.
    PR6057.R3425C4 2003
    823'.914—dc21   2002075697

'Things fall apart; the centre cannot hold;
Mere anarchy is loosed upon the world,
The blood-dimmed tide is loosed, and
    everywhere
The ceremony of innocence is drowned;
The best lack all conviction, while the worst
Are full of passionate intensity.'

'The Second Coming'
W. B. Yeats.

CHAPTER ONE

PAPERING OVER THE CRACKS

I had never seen anyone die—not even from natural causes. I suppose that is why the death of that unknown man in a country lane has always seemed for me the point at which it all started. Or do I mean finished? It certainly seemed for a long while more like an end than a beginning.

I had driven out from our home on the suburban fringes of London hoping to pick up some potatoes and apples to help us through the winter—perhaps even some meat for the freezer. There was no meat to be had but I found the rest. The farmers were only too happy to get rid of produce which they could no longer afford to pick or transport. It was a perfect day, still and clear, luminous rather than bright with that soft-edged brilliance which only comes in autumn. The broken land was a patchwork of plough and pasture, small hills and sudden valleys, with clumps of trees just beginning to turn, subtle coloured as an ancient tapestry. I turned for home, with a kind of primitive satisfaction at not going back empty handed.

'Sorry, luv. You won't get through here in a hurry.'

1

He was a small man, in a duffle coat that looked too big for him, with boots and a cloth cap tilted forward over his eyes. The tractor beside which he stood formed the last in a long line of farm vehicles which blocked the lane ahead as far as I could see. I leaned out of the car window and looked up at him.

'What's going on?'

'Demonstration,' he said succinctly. Then added grudgingly, 'Farmers and agricultural workers, demonstrating for higher prices. Can't go on feeding everyone out of our own pockets, can we?'

More cars had followed me down the lane and some of the occupants got out and came up to join us. The small man repeated his explanation.

'Well, how long are we going to be stuck here?' asked a red-faced man in a camel car-coat. 'Why isn't anyone moving? There's not much point in demonstrating here, in the middle of nowhere.'

'Don't ask me,' responded the small man. 'Ask them KBG buggers down there.' He jerked his head towards the front of the line.

There were half a dozen of us now. Someone asked,

'What have the KBG got to do with it?'

'Want to stop us, don't they. They've blocked the lane down at the junction, trying to stop us getting into the town.'

'Come on,' said the first man. 'Let's go and

2

see what's happening.'

He set off down the lane. The rest of us hesitated. One woman decided to go back and wait in her car. The rest drifted after him. I locked my door and followed them.

* * *

Further up the lane was completely blocked by men and machines. We could hear shouting and someone using a loud-hailer. It was impossible to make out the words but the tone was hectoring and the responses of the crowd angry. The lane here ran in a gulley between steep banks so the fields were several feet higher. We scrambled up and climbed through a wire strand fence. From here we could see the place where the lane met another, wider road and it was here that the confrontation was taking place. Several cars had been drawn up to form a barrier and around them stood a crowd about a hundred strong. Many of them were middle-aged and well dressed but there was a large element of younger people, including a phalanx of brawny looking young men who might have been the local rugger club. They carried Union Jacks with the initials KBG sewn onto them in white and posters proclaiming 'KEEP BRITAIN GREAT', 'STRIKERS ARE TRAITORS', 'DON'T WHINE—WORK!'

'Absolutely right!' the man in the camel coat

was saying. 'Couldn't agree more. Just wish they'd let the rest of us get on with our own business.'

I regarded the men below me as I might have regarded strange and possibly dangerous animals. I had read about the recently formed KBG, of course. At first, like many people, I had been inclined to regard them as a joke, imagining a little band of elderly and apoplectic gentlemen in a London Club. But it had become clear that there were influential people behind the organization and their propaganda was everywhere, castigating strikers, immigrants, social security benefits; the usual right-wing targets. The difference was that more and more ordinary people were voicing similar sentiments.

'Well, if you ask me,' another man said, 'They're just making things worse. Taking the law into their own hands—never works. Anyway, the farmers have got a case. If we were prepared to pay the market rate for our food perhaps we shouldn't have so many shortages.'

'I know I'd sooner pay a bit more than stand in queues for every little thing,' agreed a woman. 'When I think how you used to be able to walk into a shop and buy anything you wanted—and look at us now! Even the simplest things are luxuries.'

'Listen!' said someone.

Over the shouting I heard the sound of

approaching police sirens. Two cars drew up and several men got out and forced their way into the middle of the crowd where they began to remonstrate vigorously with the leaders of both sides. I heard the man with the megaphone shout,

'You should be with us! We support the forces of law and order!'

Eventually the crowd began to give back. One of the cars forming the blockade was moved and the first tractor inched forward.

'Better get back to our cars,' said our leader. 'Be on our way in a minute.'

We scrambled down the bank and got into our cars. The tractor ahead of me began to move. I slid the car into first gear and followed at less than a walking pace. We reached the junction. The police had cleared a way just wide enough for the single line of traffic. I had no option but to follow. On either side the KBG supporters stood resentfully, shouting slogans and waving their banners.

I don't know whether someone on one of the vehicles just ahead responded in some particularly crude or aggressive manner, but suddenly there was a roar of fury from the crowd on one side and they surged forward, sweeping aside the police. In a moment my car was surrounded by struggling bodies. Men kicked and punched, screaming at each other, and then the spanners and the pick-axe handles appeared. My car rocked as bodies thudded against it and someone, thinking I suppose that I was part of the demonstration, began to hammer on the roof with his fists. I found myself shouting incoherently, though no-one could possibly have heard me.

'Stop it. It's not my fault! Leave me alone!'

The tractor in front of me was towing a piece of farm machinery of some sort. I had no idea what it was for but it had long, curving metal spikes. As the men fought I felt certain that at any moment someone would be thrust onto one of them. Suddenly the tractor jerked forward and I thankfully pushed the car into gear again but as I began to nose ahead there was a scream from someone in front. The tractor stopped as suddenly as it had started and the crowd momentarily drew back.

The young man impaled beneath the vicious tines did not die quickly, but he was dead by the time the ambulance arrived, wailing its approach through the rapidly thinning crowd. I think I would have sat there, motionless, until they had all gone—the police, the ambulance, the angry, silent men with the ashen faces—if a young constable had not tapped on my window and asked me if I was all right.

By the time I got home Mike was there. He had the two boys in the bath and came to the head of the stairs in his shirt sleeves as I closed the front door.

'Where the hell have you been? I got home to find Betty on the door-step with the boys, wondering what on earth had happened. She brought them back after tea at the usual time and you weren't there. I've been worried about you!'

His voice was not angry, just strained and rather aggrieved. I started up the stairs towards him but half way my legs gave out under me and I sat down. He ran down and crouched beside me.

'What's happened? Have you been in an accident? You haven't smashed the car up, have you?'

I reached out to him, shaking my head and he put his arms round me. Simon, our eldest boy, appeared at the head of the stairs stark naked, saying,

'What's happened? What's the matter with Mummy?'

'It's all right, Si.' I said. 'I'm all right.'

'Go back and get dry,' Mike told him firmly. 'You'll hear all about it later.'

I managed to collect myself enough to tell him the story. He held me tightly and stroked my hair.

'Poor old Nell! It must have been terrible for you. But try not to take it to heart too much. Horrible accidents do happen. It's just that we don't usually see them.'

'This wasn't an accident, Mike,' I protested. 'Not like a road accident, or something. If those KBG people hadn't stopped the farmers from having a peaceful demonstration none of it would have happened.'

He sighed. 'Yes, I'm afraid those people are becoming a menace. I suppose something like this was inevitable. There comes a point when people won't put up with high prices and shortages and lower standards of living any longer and they have to lash out at someone. The workers lash out at management by going on strike, and the middle classes, well some of them, lash out at the strikers. But none of it's any use.'

I got up slowly and began to go downstairs.

'I'll get some supper.'

He rose too and gave a little laugh, his mood immediately lightening.

'No need! We're going to dinner with Clare and Alan. Remember?'

'Oh God, I'd forgotten!' I looked at him wearily. 'Oh, not tonight, Mike. I simply couldn't. Can't you ring up and explain?'

'But why not?' he exclaimed. 'It's just what you need. Something to take your mind off things. And it's bound to be a good meal. God knows how Clare does it, but she still manages to get hold of food we don't see from one week's end to the next.'

'Trust Clare!' I said curtly.

'Darling, I really can't see why you've taken such a dislike to her lately.' He sounded injured. 'After all, Alan is my oldest friend and we've always got on all right with them both— until lately.'

I looked up at him, standing tousled headed on the stairs with his sleeves rolled up.

'I'm sorry, love. I know you're fond of Alan—and so am I, in a way. But you must see that Clare has changed lately. She always was a bit of a bitch, but since she started working for Jocelyn Wentworth she's been unbearable. I always thought he was a horrid little man when he used to do those current affairs programmes on television, but since he became an M.P. he's been saying ghastly things, and Clare has developed into a kind of echo. I'm sick to death of hearing "Jocelyn says this" and "Jocelyn thinks that". And I don't mind betting that the reason Clare is able to provide such fabulous food is because she gets hold of it through Jocelyn on some sort of black market.'

He came down and put his arms round me again.

'Nell, darling! I think what happened today is making you take a rather—exaggerated view of things. All right, I admit Clare's politics are somewhere to the right of Genghis Khan at the moment. But she's quite harmless, you know. I think being personal assistant to a famous man has gone to her head a bit. That's all. Now,' he gave me a quick kiss, 'you go and get yourself all dressed up and I'll see the kids off to bed. We'll have a nice, cosy evening chatting to old friends and a few drinks. It's just what you need to take your mind off what

9

happened this afternoon. Hurry up, or the baby-sitter will be here before you're ready.'

I went upstairs and had a hot bath. As Mike had prophesied the act of getting ready made me feel more normal—normal enough to put on a long dress and do my hair and my make up with more than usual care, anyway. Clare was unfailingly and infuriatingly elegant with the sort of long dark hair which could be swept up into a multitude of glamorous styles. Mine went thin and ratty if I tried to grow it so I had to wear it in a short, sleek cap. I was not as tall as she was either and my figure had not been improved by the birth of the two boys. Next to Clare I always felt like the family mongrel beside a pedigree borzoi. Still, I could at least be a well-groomed mongrel!

It wasn't a very enjoyable evening, in spite of the lavish entertainment—the steak, the cream, the real coffee. (We had given that up long ago and now even instant was a luxury.) I still felt tense and desperately tired and I had a feeling that Alan and Clare were on edge too. Alan always made me feel rather nervous. He had all the attributes that make a man attractive, good looks, charm and humour and he was extremely clever. He was always the perfect host but in spite of that I had a nagging feeling that he often wondered how his friend had come to marry a mousy little creature like me.

I could have hit Mike when he began to

explain about what had happened to me that afternoon. Inevitably we were immediately plunged into a discussion of the political implications. Clare said,

'The KBG are only doing what the Government should have done years ago. It's time someone stood up to the bloody unions who are ruining the country. We need someone to see that everyone buckles down and does a decent day's work for a change.'

'It doesn't help for people to take the law into their own hands, Clare,' Mike said.

'People with a sense of responsibility can't just sit back and watch while the Marxists and the Trotskyites take over the country,' Clare said sharply. 'That's what they are aiming for. Don't be fooled, Mike. We must get together and show them we're not going to have it.'

'Do you mean by counter-demonstrations?' Mike asked. 'Look at the results that produced this afternoon.'

'There are other ways.' Clare seemed to hesitate for a moment, then went on as if the temptation to air her knowledge was too great. 'Jocelyn is working on some proposals at the moment. He suggests that every community—town, village, factory, whatever—should set up a committee to encourage everyone to make a special effort for economic recovery. Anyone who was not pulling his weight, or who was trying to cause trouble could be reported to them and—dealt with.'

11

'Dealt with? How?' Mike was gazing at Clare. She shrugged.

'The power of public opinion can make an impression, even on people like that, if it's expressed forcefully enough.'

I shivered involuntarily. 'I'm sorry, Clare, but I think that's a terrible thing to suggest. It sounds like 1984 and Big Brother and all that.'

'Oh don't exaggerate, Nell,' she said sharply. 'Don't you realize how many people are either actively trying to undermine our society by fomenting strikes and disputes, or else just sponging on the rest of us—taking social security instead of getting a job, deliberately working slowly in order to increase overtime, reporting sick every time they feel like a day off. It's time people like that were shown pretty sharply that we're not going to stand for it.'

'I know there are abuses,' Mike said reasonably, 'but surely they are a minority. Take unemployment benefit, for example. With unemployment at this level no-one can be blamed for not having a job. And it's not just the working classes either. It's hitting people like us too. Look at all the big houses up for sale and the big cars in the second hand dealers' yards.'

There was a moment's silence and then Alan said very quietly,

'You don't have to tell us, Mike.'

We stared at him. Clare said sharply,

12

'That's quite different, Alan. You're a victim of the mess these people have got us in to, that's all.'

Mike said, 'You haven't lost your job, Alan!' He spoke slowly and looked as shaken as if he had just been sacked himself.

Alan raised his head. The strain was showing plainly now around his eyes and mouth, but his tone was matter-of-fact.

'Yes, I'm afraid so. I'm working out my notice at the moment, actually. One more week and I join the ranks of the unemployed.'

'But why?' Mike asked.

Alan shrugged. 'Usual story. Recession has hit the engineering industry like everyone else, you know. They had to slim down middle management—I was one of the ones to go. Reckon I trod on a few too many toes in my haste to get to the top.'

'You mean you made the people above you nervous!' Clare said.

'Any sign of something else?' Mike asked.

Alan shook his head. 'Not so far, I'm afraid.'

There was no way of rescuing the rest of the evening. We left early, Mike having made an appointment to have lunch with Alan the next day. Getting ready for bed we went over and over the situation.

'Surely,' I said, 'he won't be out of work for long. He's always been regarded as so brilliant.'

Mike sighed. 'That may not be enough.

There just aren't any jobs going. You could be a combination of Henry Ford and Isambard Kingdom Brunel and not get a job in engineering just now.'

'What will they do?' I asked.

Mike shrugged. 'He may strike lucky, of course. And Clare's working. Thank God they haven't got any kids to worry about.'

'But that house, Mike! They've got a huge mortgage and they're in debt up to their ears for everything in it practically. Clare's salary won't cover all that.'

'Then the house will have to go, I suppose,' he replied.

'If they can sell it,' I rejoined.

We were silent for a while. I looked at Mike.

'You're not thinking it could happen to you, are you?'

'It could happen to anyone these days,' he answered; then, with an effort, 'No. No, I'm not really worried about that. Accountants are about the only people who can still make money whether the economy is growing or collapsing. No, I was thinking about Alan and Clare. If things get really bad for them, I wonder if there is any way we could help.'

'I can't somehow see Clare being very willing to accept help,' I said. 'Or Alan either for that matter.'

'Don't be uncharitable, darling,' he protested mildly.

'I'm not!' I said. 'It's just that they've always

14

been so terribly set on being "top people".'

'Well, they're not "top people" now. They're back at the bottom of the pile with a wallop. We ought to help them if we can.'

'I don't see how,' I said obstinately.

'I was thinking.' He spoke slowly. 'If the worst came to the worst, they could come and stay with us for a while, until they got back on their feet.'

I stared at him. 'Oh, Mike . . .' He met my eyes. I swallowed and said, 'All right. If the worst comes to the worst . . .'

In bed I lay for a long time flat on my back, one arm behind my head, unable to relax. At length Mike sensed my tension, rolled over and grunted enquiringly.

'I was thinking.' I said. 'Things have been bad for months now—years, really, I suppose. But we've kept on telling ourselves that it was just a bad patch; that everything would be all right again soon. Do you think it will, Mike?'

There was a pause before he answered drowsily,

'It depends on what you mean by all right, I suppose. I mean, some people would feel that things haven't really been all right since 1914.'

'I'm not going that far back,' I said irritably. 'Don't be silly.'

'Well, when were things all right, in your view? Is it the swinging sixties we want to get back to?'

'I just want to get back to a time when we

15

didn't have to stagger from one crisis to another, that's all.'

He put his arm round me. 'Don't worry, love. Things may never be quite like they were, but we'll manage.'

I sighed. 'I don't know, Mike. I've never worried about politics much. I've never really been interested. But somehow, today—that man being killed and Alan losing his job—it's made me wonder if things are ever going to be really all right again.'

I had never been the brooding type and by morning I had largely slept off my depression but I was not allowed to forget the incidents of the previous day so easily. Radio and television made a great deal of the tragedy. The man who had died had been a KBG supporter and Jocelyn Wentworth appeared on one of the news programmes to call him 'the first martyr in a long, long struggle against the forces of the far left'. Two days later a barn belonging to a farmer who had taken part in the demonstration burnt down. While the police investigated three similar fires broke out in the same area. In the last the farmhouse itself was fired and the family narrowly escaped with their lives.

I decided to talk it all over with my old school friend, Jane, who lived in a cottage on the rural fringe of what we pleased to call 'the village', though it had long ago been absorbed into the outer edges of the commuter belt.

Jane was a teacher, divorced, with three children and her image, together with Clare's, stood over my consciousness like two opposing demons. Jane lived in intense and perpetual turmoil, her cottage a shambles of books, muddy boots, damp laundry, children and animals. She worked all day, rushed home in the evening to feed the children on baked beans and bread and marmalade and was off again to attend an evening class, sit on a committee or organize a meeting. Her children had long ago ceased to expect from her one tenth of the attention that she bestowed on battered wives or immigrant families but, if the thought ever occurred to her, she probably felt that this was quite as it should be. She heartily despised women whose interest centred on their homes and dismissed with contempt my aspirations towards domestic order and beauty. In the conflict between Clare's high-powered but sterile elegance and Jane's creative disorder I was inclined to regard my life's achievements—a contented husband and two healthy children— as insignificant.

I knew now that I should have taken my teachers' advice years ago and gone to University, but I had come from a family where a degree formed no part of the kind of future projected for me. A short course at a good secretarial college and a safe job had seemed the sensible way of filling the time

17

between leaving school and getting married. It must have taken me all of ten years to recognize my mistake.

Not that I had really been discontented. It was just a faint, nagging sense of loss beneath the smooth routine of existence. Now a different kind of anxiety had begun for me; but Jane was the wrong person to go to for reassurance.

'Your trouble, Nell,' she told me earnestly, 'is that you've been going round with your head full of freezers and tumble dryers and new dining room carpets for years. Now you've got to come down out of your cosy cloud-cuckoo-land and face facts. Unless we do something about it we shall have a fascist government in this country within a couple of years. If you're really worried enough to do something there's a meeting you can come to next Wednesday.'

I made an excuse, a reasonable enough one, but I could see she did not believe me. I had no intention of getting involved in politics. I had always been able to see too many sides to any question to commit myself to an ideology. Around me, however, opinions were polarizing rapidly. Acrimonious disputes broke out in the food queues and Mike told me that it was the same on the 8.17 to Waterloo.

'It's almost reached the stage,' he said, 'when *Telegraph* readers and *Guardian* readers stand and glare at each other from opposite ends of the platform!'

Clare, we learned, had gone off on a nation-wide speaking tour with Jocelyn Wentworth. Alan was coping on his own.

It must have been around then that the dustmen went on strike. We took to burning as much rubbish as we could, but still the plastic bags of bottles and tins accumulated outside the back door, until we had to start dumping them at the bottom of the garden. News bulletins showed city streets piled with rubbish, with rats scurrying amongst them. Jocelyn Wentworth, among others, urged the use of troops. Several of his meetings broke up in violent disorder. Then KBG units moved in in several areas and began clearing the rubbish. There were confrontations with strike pickets and police reinforcements were rushed in. Eventually, strike leaders agreed to allow troops to clear the worst areas and Jocelyn Wentworth claimed a victory for the KBG.

The Government, which was being firm to the point of lunacy with the dustmen, decided to give in to the farmers, and food prices made another upward spiral. Milk and cheese, which we had come to regard as staples now that meat was so short, began to seem like luxuries. We were not going hungry, but money that a year ago might have been set aside for a holiday or to replace the car now went on housekeeping and even so I had to plan every meal with great care.

The autumn passed. Clare came back from her tour and we invited her and Alan to dinner, but it was not a success. Alan was bitter and sardonic and Clare could talk of nothing but Jocelyn and the KBG. He had had to sell his car, which he had always regarded like part of himself. She, however, still had hers. A few weeks later he phoned to say that they had put the house on the market. I began to regard the future with growing dismay.

Three weeks before Christmas the electricity power workers went on strike.

CHAPTER TWO

DISINTEGRATION

Oddly enough, it was rather a good Christmas. Mike managed to get hold of a chicken, though he would not tell me how or what he paid for it. The turkey which I had hoarded in the freezer for months had to be eaten at the beginning of the strike, before it became unusable along with the rest of the stock which had been our cushion against increasing shortages. With the power only coming on for three hours out of each twenty-four we were lucky to be able to cook our Christmas dinner only a couple of hours later than usual. Afterwards we huddled around the gas fire and, deprived of the soporific comfort of the television, sang carols and told stories. The boys found the loss of television the hardest part of the strike to bear and over the holiday Mike and I found ourselves playing with them more than we had done for years. It was that, together with the sense of being a close unit standing together against the faceless powers outside, that made it a good Christmas. I only wished that my parents, who lived in Wales, could be with us but in the circumstances of that winter long journeys were to be avoided unless absolutely essential.

At the beginning of the new year Alan phoned and asked Mike to meet him. Later that evening Mike returned, grim-faced and uneasy.

'What did he want?' I asked.

'They've sold the house.'

'Well, that's good news, isn't it?'

He shook his head. 'Not really. They didn't get anything like the proper value for it. Alan didn't tell me the exact figures but it's pretty clear they must have dropped several thousand on what they originally paid. He says it'll just about clear the mortgage. The man who bought it is some kind of property dealer.'

'What are they going to do now?'

'That's just the point.' He came and sat by me on the settee. 'Alan says they've been looking for somewhere else for weeks and there's nowhere. They haven't got the capital left to put down a deposit on another house, even if they could find something at the right price, and you can't find rented accommodation at any price. He says he's been told that there are hundreds of quite respectable families squatting in empty houses because they're in the same position as him and Clare.'

I looked at him. 'I suppose you want them to come here?'

He returned my look with a kind of humble appeal. 'I did tell Alan weeks ago that they could come, if they needed to.'

I sighed deeply. The prospect of living with Alan's defensive cynicism and Clare's fanaticism appalled me.

'I suppose they'll have to come then,' I said.

He drew me to him. 'I know it's not going to be much fun for you, love. But we can't let them down, can we? And I expect it will only be for a few weeks.'

That was an expectation reiterated with almost embarrassing frequency by Alan and Clare when they moved in a week later. In fact, Clare was so dogmatic in her assertion that I began to wonder whether she had any definite prospect in mind; perhaps through some intervention from Jocelyn Wentworth. But when I tried to discuss the idea with her she was evasive. She often came in late or spent whole evenings in the room we had given them typing, while Alan sat with us, silent and depressed. I had the impression that she was immersing herself in her work to the exclusion of all else, even Alan—perhaps especially Alan. He went off religiously every morning with Mike and spent the day combing the offices and pubs of the city in search of useful contacts. I knew that his season ticket had run out and suspected that Mike was paying his fares but I said nothing. It was a relief to have the house to myself during the day at least.

One evening early in the new term the boys came home wearing KBG badges. They had been handed out by someone who had come to talk to them at school. It took me some time to persuade them to take them off.

As soon as I could find an opportunity I telephoned Jane and asked if I could go over to see her that evening. I had to talk to someone and I knew it would be worse than useless to discuss it in front of Clare and Alan. Besides, I was glad to be out of the house for an evening, even though it meant a longish walk through the unlit streets. Petrol was far too precious now to be used for that sort of thing.

Jane was sitting at the table in her cluttered kitchen, marking books by the light of a single candle amid a litter of unwashed cups, somebody's stamp collection and a half-dismantled radio. A line of damp washing hung above her head and the sink was stacked with dirty dishes. She looked up, pushing her straight dark hair back off her heavy pale face. She never wore make-up and only washed her hair when she remembered it.

'Hullo,' she said. 'Make yourself at home. I must finish these, then I'll get some coffee.'

I removed the cat and a pair of dirty wellingtons from the chair opposite her and sat down.

'I'm sorry to come and bother you. I know you're always so busy.'

'Don't be daft. I'm never so busy that I can't find time to see my friends.' She was continuing to mark books as she spoke.

I said. 'I've got to talk to you about something.'

'Oh?'

I glared at the top of her head. Just for once I needed her undivided attention. I could hear her children arguing noisily over a game in the other room. How often had they felt a similar but much greater irritation, I wondered. Then I felt a pang of guilt. What right had I, with nothing to do but care for my home and children, to demand anything of Jane—least of all something as precious to her as time?

I said, 'Shall I make the coffee?'

She looked up. 'I thought you wanted to talk.'

'Well, I can talk and make coffee at the same time, can't I?'

'O.K.' she said, returning to the books. 'Carry on. You know where everything is.'

I busied myself with the coffee, surreptitiously washing a few of the dirty dishes while I waited for the kettle to boil. I had annoyed Jane before by trying to do such things for her. After a moment she growled,

'Stop it, Nell! You're trying to shame me with your damn middle-class cleanliness again, aren't you? Go and be house-proud in your own house.'

'Don't be silly, Jane!' I exclaimed. 'I'm only trying to help.'

'Well, don't.' She pushed the books away from her and looked at me. 'Come on, what is it you want to talk about?'

I took the coffee over to the table and told her about the KBG badges. Her expression changed instantly.

'Good God! I didn't realise you meant something like this when you said you wanted to discuss something important. The damn cheek of the man. Bringing politics into the school. Right. We'll soon settle his hash. What you have to do is to write to the Area Education Officer and complain that your children are being politically indoctrinated— and get as many other Mums as you can to write as well.'

'Oh I don't know, Jane,' I protested. 'I think "politically indoctrinated" is a bit strong. I don't want to get the poor man sacked. The boys have always got on very well there.'

Jane leaned forward. 'Nell, you have got to

stop being a political baby! Don't you realize that this country is on the verge of a civil war? "Poor man"! The KBG is the single most dangerous influence in the country today. They are deliberately fomenting unrest and when things get bad enough they will put in their own Fascist government.'

'Oh Jane, how could they?'

'You don't believe me? You don't realize how the very laws and institutions they claim to be defending could be used to put them in power. Well, you just sit back and watch it happen.'

'Look,' I said unhappily, 'you know I'm no good at this sort of thing. All I want is to stop the children being involved.'

'O.K.' She leaned forward. 'Let's stick to the children. Has it occurred to you that any government could take your children away from you any time it wanted?'

'Oh don't be ridiculous!'

'It's not ridiculous. It's fact. Listen. The local authority can take into care any child it suspects of being at risk. Right? And only last year we had a report by a Committee of Inquiry stating that the authority should act immediately upon the "slightest suspicion" that a child is in danger.'

'But we needed something like that. There were so many cases of children not being taken away and then being beaten or starved to death. The child has to come first.'

'Yes, I know,' she exclaimed. 'But don't you see how a totalitarian government, of whatever complexion, could use that? Suppose one of your boys fell out of a tree or put his arm through a window. How easily someone could suspect that you had been knocking him about. Or take a family where the father is unemployed. Who can keep five or six kids adequately fed and clothed on social security these days? You mark my words. We shall see children in those circumstances being taken into care before this winter's over.'

'But that's not the same thing,' I protested. 'That's a case of real need.'

'But it's the idea I'm getting at. The KBG are trying to get hold of the kids. You've seen that. Now it's talks in schools and badges and a lot of jingoistic claptrap. In six months' time it could be by taking thousands of them into care.'

I sat gazing at her for a moment. The idea was so horrifying that my mind refused to give it credence. In the end I said,

'Well, I think you're taking it a bit far.'

She shrugged and drew the pile of books towards her. 'Suit yourself. But if you care about what happens to your children—specially about what happens to their minds—you write that letter.'

I wrote the next day. I also made a point of meeting the boys from school and chatting to some of the other mothers. One or two were annoyed about the talk, a few others strongly in favour of it. No-one was sufficiently disturbed to want to take any action.

When the children came out Simon had a rip in his anorak.

'Oh Simon,' I exclaimed. 'How did you do that?'

He shrugged and did not look at me. 'Some of us were fighting the KBG boys and one of them grabbed my coat and ripped it.'

'What do you mean, the KBG boys?'

He gave me a look which suggested that the answer was self-evident. 'The boys who are wearing the badges. Some of us took them off and the others didn't. Then some of them started shouting things at us—so we fought them.'

Two days later Clare came home unexpectedly in the middle of the afternoon. She came into the kitchen and said,

'Nell, would you come into the lounge, please. I want to talk to you.'

I said, 'Hallo. What are you doing back so early? Would you like some tea? The power's on.'

She looked at me, her lips tightening. She had taken to wearing her hair very tightly drawn back from her face and in a pleat at the back of her head and her clothes, too, had become severely elegant rather than pretty. She looked, I thought, as if she were in uniform. She said,

'I haven't come back because I've finished work. I've been sent to talk to you.' And she moved away into the living room.

I washed my hands and followed her, drying them on the kitchen towel. She had seated herself in front of the gas fire with her slim legs elegantly crossed.

'Well?' I said.

She looked at me. 'Nell, I've been asked to give you a bit of advice. Some people think that you're being rather foolish, and you could end up by making yourself extremely unpopular.'

I dropped the towel onto the back of a chair and sat down opposite her.

'I haven't the faintest idea what you are talking about.'

'Did you write to the Area Education Officer complaining about the talk at the school the other day?'

'Yes, I did. I think it was an awful thing to do, trying to involve kids in all this.' I stopped and looked at her. 'How did you know I had written?'

She shrugged the question aside. 'Never mind that for the moment.'

'But I do mind!' I overrode her angrily. 'How did you know?'

For a moment she hesitated. Then she drew in a sharp breath and said crisply,

'All right. Let's get it absolutely straight. You must realize that Jocelyn is—well,

29

associated with the KBG.'

'You can hardly miss that,' I said, dryly.

'What you perhaps don't realize is that he is a very important person in the KBG organization—both nationally and in this particular area.'

'And Jocelyn doesn't like people criticizing the KBG.'

'Jocelyn knows that the only chance this country has is to unite behind the KBG and stand up to the people who are trying to undermine our society.'

'So I suppose you told him that I objected to my children being recruited into—into an organization they can't possibly understand?'

Clare shook her head calmly. 'No, Nell. I didn't tell him anything. I didn't need to. He's been getting reports about you from several sources.'

'What sources?' I felt suddenly chilled.

'I don't know them all. I only know that you have been writing letters and trying to persuade other people to write them too. And then, of course, there's your association with Jane Grant.'

'For God's sake!' I exploded. 'What has Jane got to do with it?'

'Oh don't be naive, Nell!' Her voice was sharp. 'Everyone knows that Jane is a left-wing agitator. Whenever there is a meeting or a committee or any function where the Marxists and the Trots are in control, there she is, in the

30

thick of it.'

'Clare! Will you stop putting meaningless labels on people? Jane believes in certain causes—good ones: ones I wish I had the courage or the—the unselfishness to do something about. She isn't a Marxist or a Trot!'

Clare rose and stood looking down at me.

'Well, I'm afraid you don't really understand what's going on here. So just be advised, will you? If you go on spreading anti-KBG propaganda you are going to be very unpopular with a lot of people who have a lot of influence and that could be very difficult for you—and for Mike and the children. It's already making things awkward for me and Alan, but I suppose you would say we have no right to complain about that. Anyway, I've done what I was asked to do, so now I'll get back. Just think about it, will you?'

The back door crashed open. Instantly I could hear Tim sobbing and Simon shouting, 'Mum! Mum! Come here, Quick!' I rushed into the kitchen. Tim stood on the doormat. His coat was torn and muddy and his nose was bleeding. His face was streaked with mud and tears. I went down on my knees and put my arms round him.

'Timmy, darling, what happened?'

Simon answered. 'Some KBG boys beat him up. They were waiting for us on the way home from school. They said you'd been writing letters to the Headmaster complaining about the badges and that made us Arch-Enemy No. 1. They didn't hurt me much because I was too tough for them, but they knocked Timmy down. I tried to stop them, but there were six of them onto us two.'

I held Tim close to me, knowing that the blood from his nose must be getting onto my jersey, and looked up to see Clare standing in the doorway.

'If Alan wasn't Mike's best friend I'd never have had you in this house in the first place,' I said viciously. 'But now you'd better start looking for somewhere else to go, before I kick you out into the street.'

A few days later two very polite young men knocked at my door and asked me to identify myself. To my annoyance the sight of the KBG badges in their lapels made my heart thump and my knees tremble. They carried copies of the electoral roll and explained that a number of empty houses in the area had been taken over by squatters and they were checking to make sure that only the rightful owners were in occupation. I wondered, but did not ask, what they would do if they found some squatters. They wanted to know if we had anyone else in the house. When I mentioned Clare's name their manner underwent a subtle change and I could see that it was known to them.

Mike came in late that evening and

announced that the railwaymen had started an unofficial go-slow. Alan had come home early and at supper he said,

'I left Town a bit earlier than usual today. There didn't seem to be much point in hanging around, with the trains likely to stop at any moment. I took a walk round by our house— just to have a look at it, you know. I think there are squatters in there.'

'What!' Clare exclaimed.

'Well, there are definitely people in there,' Alan said.

'How do you know they are squatters?' Mike asked. 'Couldn't they just be the new owners?'

Alan shook his head. 'There was a dreadful old heap of a car outside and half a dozen grubby children in the garden. They look like squatters to me.'

I said, as gently as I could, 'After all, it isn't your responsibility, Alan. It isn't actually your house any more.'

Clare's voice was harsh. 'As far as I'm concerned that is still our house. We were virtually robbed by being forced to sell it to that dreadful man and one day we're going back to it. Meanwhile I'm not having it turned into a slum by squatters.'

'What I don't understand is,' I said, 'if you sold it, why isn't it occupied?'

Alan sighed and shook his head. 'I'm afraid the man we sold it to had no intention of using

33

it. He's a property speculator, buying up houses at knock-down prices from people like us and hoping to re-sell them when things improve.'

'He would have looked more at home with a horse and cart than behind the wheel of that Rover,' Clare added bitterly. 'He has obviously made money on some black market operation and now he is putting it into property. Well he and his like have got a nasty shock coming to them.'

'What do you mean?' Mike asked.

'When we . . . when we get a proper government in this country people like that will get what they deserve. And it won't be much longer now.'

'Meanwhile houses are left empty and become an open invitation to squatters,' Alan's voice was flat and tired. I had a feeling that he was coming to the end of his tether.

'You can hardly blame people, I suppose,' Mike said. 'If they're wandering the streets homeless and jobless and afraid that their children will be taken away from them and the family broken up, it must seem unjust that there are houses standing empty.'

'That's typical of your type, Mike!' Clare said sharply. 'Typical wet liberal thinking! Don't you understand that our society is founded on the idea of private property? Once you start saying that in certain circumstances the laws of property can be ignored then you

34

open the way to total disintegration. Anyway,' she rose, ignoring Mike's attempt to argue, 'I'm not seeing it happen to us.'

She left the room and we heard her lift the telephone extension in the kitchen. There was a silence. Mike and I exchanged glances and then looked at Alan. He stared at his plate. We both knew that he had lost any power or influence over Clare's actions in relation to Jocelyn Wentworth and the KBG.

Shortly Clare came back. She looked composed and satisfied, like an efficient secretary who has just dealt with a tricky problem for her boss.

'They'll go tonight,' she said briefly.

Alan looked at her. 'What have you done?'

She returned his gaze serenely and spoke in a detached voice, as if to an importunate child. 'Don't worry about it. Those people will be moved on tonight. I've spoken to someone who deals with these things.'

'You mean you've set your KBG thugs onto them!' I surprised myself by the anger in my voice.

Clare returned my look composedly but I did not miss the glint in her eyes.

'What makes you call them thugs? Have you ever seen one of them use force, except in response to force? Have any of them ever been less than courteous to you?'

I glared at her, knowing I was on difficult ground. 'I know what I've seen on the television. And I'm not such a fool as to imagine that those people will move out for a "courteous" request.'

Clare shrugged. 'Then that's their own stupid fault, isn't it.'

Mike said, 'Clare, there are women and children in the house. Surely they have a right to shelter somewhere.'

'Not in my house,' Clare said crisply.

It had been a depressing day. There had been fighting in the bread queue when the baker sold out. I had spent hours queuing for basic essentials and returned to a house that now seemed permanently cold without power to operate the pump on the central heating. When the electricity came on I watched the television. From all over the country came stories of demonstrations and counter-demonstrations, many of them breaking up in violence. Members of the Government and the TUC were interviewed hurrying in and out of meetings, uttering the usual formulae. In many quarters the call was going up for the Government to resign.

I had managed to get some stewing lamb and had made it into a casserole with some lentils. It seemed to me a tasty and nourishing meal, even if the meat was mostly fat and bone, and I had put it on the table with a real sense of achievement; but obviously no-one was enjoying it. Alan looked pinched and weary and Clare's cool self-possession had congealed into frigid hostility. Mike was depressed and touchy. Even the children, who had had until recently a boisterous disregard for adult moods and temperaments, had developed over the last few weeks a canny awareness and were silent too. Until Simon said,

'Mum, this meat's horrid. It's all fat.'

His voice had the childish whine which he put on when he felt he was being hard done by, a tone guaranteed to annoy me at the best of times.

'Cut the fat off and eat the rest,' I said icily.

He pushed several pieces of meat to the side of his plate. 'I'm not eating any of it. It's disgusting!'

I leaned across the table and pushed the meat back to the centre of the plate with my knife. 'You will eat it, Simon, if I have to push it down your ungrateful throat. You're lucky to get any meat at all.'

'I don't want any at all. I'd rather go without than eat that muck!' His voice was hoarse with anger and suppressed tears.

I went round the table and seized him by the scruff of the neck, pulling him out of his chair. I was shaking with fury and distress.

'Do you realize, you horrible little boy, that I stood in a queue in the cold for half an hour this morning to get that meat for you? Do you realize that there are children not very far from here who haven't got a hot meal at all tonight? Children who haven't even got a home to go to? Now you either eat that food or you can leave the table now and go straight to bed. You're going to have to learn to eat what's put before you. I can't cater to your fads and fancies any longer.'

I shoved him roughly back into his chair and resumed my place, panting, ashamed at my outburst yet still bitterly certain that I was in the right. Simon was crying and saying,

'I'm not going to eat it! I shall be sick if I eat it!'

Mike said sternly, 'Your mother's quite right, Simon. We can't waste good food. Nobody is going to make you eat the fat but you must eat the rest of it. Now get on with it and stop that noise.'

For a moment Simon sat staring from one to the other of us, his face red and tear streaked. Then he pushed away his plate, got up and stamped out of the room. I was about to call after him but Mike put a hand on my arm and said,

'Let him go. If he goes to bed hungry tonight perhaps it will teach him a lesson. I'll go and see if he wants to come down and apologize later on.'

In the silence which followed Clare, who had been toying with her own meal, quietly but decisively pushed what was left to the side of her plate and laid down her knife and fork.

I looked at her and saw the subtle, sardonic

38

challenge in her eyes. Speechlessly I turned to Mike.

He said quietly, 'Not good enough for you, Clare?'

She smiled. 'Well, I think we have to admit it's not one of your best efforts, Nell. I thought you were a little bit hard on poor Simon. It's funny. I've always thought of you as a good cook.'

I found that I was gripping my knife and fork so tightly that they were visibly trembling. With a great effort I laid them down quietly on my plate and clenched my hands on the edge of the table.

'Clare, you have been living here for three weeks. I know that Alan is out of work and I know that we invited you, but you have not once offered to give me anything towards the house-keeping. I don't know what you earn, but I know that you still run your car and you always seem to have plenty of petrol for it. Also I don't mind betting that you get a good lunch every day with Jocelyn Wentworth. I'm sure he doesn't want for anything, even these days. Well, some of us don't have those advantages. It was difficult enough to manage when there were only four of us. It's been a nightmare trying to feed six. I've asked you before to go. Now I'm telling you. After tonight I don't want you in this house again!'

I sat still, with my head down, not daring to look at any of them; knowing what a blow I must have dealt Alan, fearing that I had hurt Mike too. In silence Clare rose and went to the door. There, she turned back and said, apparently to no-one in particular,

'Don't worry about looking for me. I know where I can go.

Alan got to his feet and blundered after her. We heard them go upstairs and the bedroom door slammed. I looked up and suddenly saw Timmy's anxious little face, the eyes huge and round, staring at me. He had carefully cleared up every scrap of food on his plate. I caught him up into my arms and wept into the soft angle of his neck.

Mike came and put his arms round both of us.

'I'm sorry, Mike,' I wept. 'I'm sorry!'

'It's all right,' he soothed me. 'She deserved it, and I'd warned Alan today that they'd have to find somewhere else.'

He went to the sideboard and brought me a glass of the brandy we had been hoarding since our last holiday abroad. I sipped it and got control of myself.

'Mike, go up and see Simon, will you? Ask him if he wants to come down and have some pudding. Tell him it's apple crumble.'

Simon came down and we finished our meal in an atmosphere of family closeness which was accentuated by the absence of Alan and Clare. As we were about to leave the table we heard the front door close and after a moment

Alan came slowly into the room and sat down silently in front of the fire. I exchanged glances with Mike and put another serving of pie onto a plate. Then I took the children up to bed. Mike came up to find me later and we sat on the edge of our bed, huddled together with the eiderdown round our shoulders.

'Alan says he thinks Clare's left him for good.'

'Oh God! Is it my fault, do you think?'

'No, darling,' he hugged me reassuringly. 'He says it's been brewing up ever since he lost his job. Clare's one of these people who can't tolerate failure.'

'Where has she gone?' I asked.

Mike shrugged. 'She wouldn't tell him, because she said she didn't want him going round there making scenes. But he thinks she's gone to Jocelyn.'

'You don't mean that she's having an affair with him, do you? He's a ghastly man, old enough to be her grandfather, almost.'

'He's a very successful man, to Clare's way of thinking. Famous, well-off, influential—for the time being, anyway. She's hero-worshipped him for years. Alan doesn't know whether it's anything more than that, but he says she's become quite obsessive about him lately.'

'Well, we know that,' I agreed.

'Anyway,' Mike concluded, 'that's where Alan thinks she is, and he doesn't think she'll come back.'

'Poor Alan!' I whispered.

He hugged me again. 'You won't mind if he stays on with us?'

'No, of course not. I don't mind Alan.'

The next morning Alan did not appear at breakfast. Mike went to investigate and reported,

'He's all right, but he says he isn't going to bother coming up to Town today. There isn't a lot of point, really, especially with the railwaymen playing silly devils. God knows what time I shall get back tonight. You'll have to expect me when you see me.' He gave me a quick peck. 'Keep an eye on poor old Alan, will you?'

'Yes, I will,' I promised. 'I'll take him up some breakfast shortly.'

He waved and the front door slammed behind him. I began to clear the table and put the kettle on for fresh tea. Alan came in in his dressing-gown. His hair was ruffled and his face seemed to have grown thinner overnight. I guessed he had not slept. He dropped into his chair and muttered an apology for not being dressed.

'It's all right,' I told him. 'Actually, I was going to bring you some breakfast in bed.'

I went into the hall to shout to the boys to hurry up. 'You've still got the guinea pigs to feed before school.' Then I switched on the transistor radio in the kitchen and tuned it to Radio 3. The music helped to take the raw edge off the atmosphere. I made another pot of tea and fresh toast for Alan. He accepted it and ate almost as if he was unaware of what he was doing, his eyes fixed blankly on the centre of the table. The boys clattered downstairs and out into the garden to attend to the animals. I was occupied for a while organizing mid-morning drinks and biscuits and finding coats and gloves and school bags. Then they were gone and I was alone with Alan.

I said, 'Alan, I'm sorry about last night—and about Clare. If what I said was—well, the last straw...'

He looked up and shook his head. 'It wasn't that. She'd have gone anyway. But I had a feeling she was—waiting for something.'

'What do you mean?'

'I don't know. I think she'd made up her mind to leave me weeks ago, but she wasn't quite ready. I knew it wouldn't be long.' He met my eyes, and said wryly, 'Thanks for putting up with us.'

I swallowed. 'I haven't minded having you, Alan. You know that. It's just that Clare has become so—so strange. All this KBG business. Mike says I'm silly to take it seriously, but it frightens me, Alan.'

For a moment his fare lost the loose lines of dejection and became alert. 'Mike's wrong, Nell. The KBG is no joke, believe me. In the days when—when Clare and I were—closer, she used to tell me things. That's when it all

43

started to go wrong. I couldn't go along with some of the things she told me about.'

'What sort of things?'

He dropped his eyes and shook his head and in the pause the radio announcer began to read the news.

'It has just been announced from 10, Downing Street after an all-night meeting of the Cabinet that the Government has decided to resign. New elections will be held as soon as possible, but the date has not yet been chosen.

'Immediately following this announcement comes news of a new political party, to be known as The National Unity Party. A statement from the party's headquarters in London names several prominent people as founder-members and states that the party intends to fight as many seats at the forth-coming election as possible. Among those named were . . .'

We listened in silence to the list of names, looking into each other's faces. One of the names was that of Jocelyn Wentworth. Others were also associated with the KBG. Several belonged to prominent figures inside and outside of politics whose involvement came as a surprise to me.

'You see . . . ?' Alan said.

I nodded. The radio announcer was talking about chaotic conditions on the railways, with drivers walking out in the middle of journeys and leaving train-loads of angry commuters stranded. There had been ugly scenes at several stations when passengers attempted to force drivers to continue.

The phone rang. Automatically I went to answer it. It was Clare asking coolly to speak to Alan. I called him and went back to the kitchen. He came back quite quickly and sat down again at the table.

'So that's it. I knew she was waiting for something.'

'What do you mean?'

Alan spoke in a faint parody of Clare's voice. 'Now that Jocelyn is standing for Parliament he needs her with him all the time. They are leaving for his constituency today.'

I sat down opposite him. 'Has she gone for the political involvement, the excitement of being where the power is—or is it for Jocelyn himself?'

He gave me a wry, lop-sided grin. 'I think the two are inseparable as far as she's concerned, Nell. Jocelyn is her guru, the Messiah, the Führer. I don't think she's ever questioned anything he's told her.'

'Do you think he'll get in?' I asked.

He lifted both hands and shook his head in a gesture of helplessness. 'I've no more idea than you have. The way things are at the moment anything could happen at this election.'

'But suppose a lot of his people get in. I mean, is there any chance at all that they could form a government?'

'I shouldn't think it's likely but there's no doubt that all this unrest has produced a tremendous right-wing backlash and there are a lot of people who would give anything for a "strong" government to put an end to all the uncertainty. They could end up holding the balance of power.'

'And then what?'

'Then God help us all!' His shoulders sagged and his eyes became fixed again. The wry grin touched his lips. 'Specially me. Once Clare gets the taste of real power she'll never let go again.'

I hesitated. Questions seemed impertinent and yet was it not still more heartless to remain silent?

'Do you still love her, Alan?'

I thought at first he had not heard me, or chose to ignore the question. Then he took a deep breath.

'There was a time, Nell, when I thought she was the most perfect creature I'd ever met. Her face, her figure, her mind, her whole style and manner of being—impeccable! When I married her it was like owning a—a Ming vase or a painting by Renoir. And she was good at everything, Nell—I mean, everything. Clare may have looked cool, but she certainly wasn't cold.'

'And do you still feel like that about her?'

'I feel,' he said heavily, 'as if someone,

46

perhaps it was me, had taken a pot of paint and defaced the picture, or smashed the vase. It no longer exists as the thing it once was.'

I looked at him and remembered the witty, smart Alan with his beautiful wife who had once made me feel inadequate; and I put out my hand and laid it on his. He glanced up at me with a trace of the old, humorous charm and then he put my hand against his cheek and held it there tightly for a moment. Then he got up quickly, without looking at me, and went out of the room.

I thought it best to leave him to himself for a while and got on with my work. When I heard the front door dose I had an impulse to run and call him back, but there seemed no real point in doing so. There was, after all, nothing to occupy him in the house. When he did not come back for lunch I guessed that he had not liked to impose on me for an extra meal, and felt guilty about my outburst the previous evening.

The day passed and the children came home from school. With darkness there was still no sign of Alan. I wondered if he had changed his mind and gone up to Town after all. Perhaps he would come back with Mike. The radio still spoke of trains cancelled and delayed, so I gave the boys their meal and read to them until bedtime. There was still no sign of either of the men. I ate myself and settled down to wait in the glow of the gas-fire. It seemed a waste to burn candles now unless I really needed to see.

Presently it occurred to me to wonder if Alan had made his bed. That had been one job which Clare had previously taken care of and I had always avoided going into their room as far as possible. I went upstairs and knew as soon as I entered the room that Alan would not be coming back. Previously the room had surprised me when I had looked in by its untidiness, as if Clare's obsessive neatness somehow failed to embrace this temporary refuge. Now no sign of occupation remained, except for a letter lying on the dressing-table. It was so obvious, so necessary a part of the scenario, that it seemed ridiculous that I had waited all day before finding it.

'Dear Nell,

I know this will seem cowardly and ungrateful of me, but I can't stand the thought of explanations and arguments just now. Clare and I have imposed on you far too long already and now that she is gone I can't go on trying to fool myself that the old life is just around the corner and all I need is a lucky break. I know now that the old days are never coming back—not for me, at any rate.

Don't go jumping to the conclusion that I'm about to do myself in or anything equally dramatic. I'm much too conventional for that. There must be someone, somewhere who wants an engineer—even if it's only to mend a broken ploughshare. Anyway, I'm going to look.

Bless you both for all you've done. I don't need to explain how I feel about it to Mike— just give him my love, will you.

I've left one or two suits and things in the wardrobe. They are too heavy to carry about with me, and leaving them there gives me a feeling that I shall come back for them, one day. I hope it will be soon.

Love,
Alan.

I took the letter downstairs and sat by the fire again, trying to imagine where Alan might have gone. North, perhaps, to one of the great industrial cities? I pictured him tramping the streets with the faceless thousands already searching for work. There seemed no sense in that. 'Ploughshares' he had said. Perhaps he had gone into the country then, searching the villages and the quiet market towns. How had he travelled? On a crowded train, with no certainty that it would ever reach its destination? By coach, maybe, if he had the money for his fare. Or had he hitched? Alan, who had parted so unwillingly with his Audi only a couple of months before. I sighed and shivered, in spite of the fire. Mike would be upset, that was certain. I knew that Alan, the old school friend, the one remaining link with childhood and adolescence, was important to him in a primitive, tribal way which I only half understood. He would worry about him, perhaps even want to look for him; but where could you start looking?

I fetched the radio and switched it on. It had suddenly occurred to me that it was almost nine o'clock and I had had no word from Mike. I was used to him being delayed, but he usually managed to telephone. However, I comforted myself with the thought that he could be stuck on a train somewhere, miles from the nearest phone.

The news came on. I turned up the volume, expecting further information about the election and the National Unity Party.

'Four people have died—and more than thirty were injured, some of them seriously, in the riot which broke out in Waterloo Station this evening. Trouble began when angry commuters tried to force the driver of a train which had just arrived to return to his cab and take the train out again. The driver refused and a scuffle broke out in which the driver was hit over the head. Other railway workers came to his assistance and the drivers of two trains which had been about to leave left their cabs in protest. Fighting spread all through the station, which was packed with people trying to get home after leaving work. Gates to platforms were forced open and passengers occupied trains and even threatened to drive them themselves. It took police more than an hour to restore order. Of the four men who died, one was a railway porter who was killed when one of the gates collapsed and two others were passengers who were crushed by the pressure of the crowd as they attempted to reach the trains. The fourth man is believed to have fallen between two carriages onto the live rail. Names are not being released until next of kin have been informed. The injured have been taken to St Thomas's hospital.'

It took me a long time to get through to the hospital. Mike was not among the injured. I knelt before the fire and thrust my fists against my mouth to stifle the howl of terror that rose in my throat. He could still be on his way home! I repeated the words aloud. What had happened when it was all over? Had the trains run in the end? I turned back to the radio which had continued to talk unheeded. Jocelyn Wentworth was being interviewed about his return to politics. The interviewer probed the connection between the KBG and the National Unity Party. Jocelyn insisted that there was none, but added that the NUP embodied the same yearning for effective government and a rebirth of national pride which had produced the KBG movement. Listening with half my mind, the other half willing the sound of his latchkey in the door, I heard the interviewer say,

'It has been suggested, Mr Wentworth, that

men wearing KBG badges in their lapels were among those who started the trouble at Waterloo Station tonight. It has even been suggested on this, as on previous occasions, that KBG members have acted as agents provocateurs. Have you any comment to make about that?'

'Of course,' Jocelyn's familiar voice was urbane and slightly husky. (Why did I always think of him as Jocelyn? Because of Clare I supposed. I had met him once through her and found him waspish and self-absorbed. My brain was working hard on a conscious, almost verbal level, in order to contain the panic beneath.) 'Of course, there is absolutely no foundation for the latter accusation. May I emphasize that the KBG movement, as it has come to be called, is not a centralized organization. It is simply a spontaneous coming together of people in many areas who are fed up with seeing this country sliding further and further into decline simply because the majority have been too weak and spineless to stand up to the subversive elements who want to see our society totally undermined. If some people who back this movement were enraged at the prospect of yet more disruption and infuriated by the fact that a few dissidents can prevent the rest of us from getting on with the jobs which we want to do, I can only sympathize with them. I deplore the results of their action, of course, but I sympathize with the frustration which produced it.'

I switched off the radio. Outside, the street was dark and silent. I tried to telephone the station but there was no reply.

The police came about half an hour later. They had brought my next-door neighbour, Molly Randall, with them. Normally we seldom spoke to each other but now she oozed sympathy and self-importance. I felt neither surprise or terror at their appearance. The knowledge was already contained inside me. Their arrival was merely confirmation. I led them into the lounge and sat as before by the fire. That night I could not seem to get warm. I half listened to their careful, anxious voices. Mike had fallen between two carriages when the pressure of people forcing their way onto the platform had pushed him over the edge. The train had been about to leave. In the confusion no-one had seen him fall. His body had not been discovered until after the train had pulled out . . .

Molly fussed around making tea. The policemen stood awkwardly, unsure how to take my silence. I got rid of them eventually and went upstairs to the room where the children slept. Simon lay on his back, arms and legs spread-eagled; Tim was curled into a neat bundle. Both breathed so quietly that I had to strain my ears to hear it. We had had to move them both into one room to make room for Alan and Clare, so the beds were quite close

53

together. I knelt down between them and stretched out my arms so that I could touch them both. Simon rolled onto his side and sighed. It was cold and after a few minutes my arms began to ache and my legs were cramped. I lifted my head and opened my mouth in a great, soundless howl of despair. Again and again I screamed silently within myself. Then I bent my head and heard my tears dropping on the carpet. I wept, as I had screamed, silently, so as not to wake the children. Morning and its explanations would come too soon for all of us.

CHAPTER THREE

STATE OF EMERGENCY

I do not think very often of the weeks which followed Mike's death and when I do the memories are vague. I am not sure whether this is a deliberate refusal to recall or whether my mind genuinely has not retained a clear picture. Nature, at least in retrospect, performs its own anaesthesia. I know Jane more or less took me over. I had become overnight not just a friend but that far more deserving cause—'someone in trouble'. Jane dealt with all the formalities, arranged the funeral, coped with the children and began to reorganize my life. The only thing she did not do, could not do, being Jane, was to take me in her arms and let me sob my heart out. There was no-one who could do that for me.

Alan had disappeared without trace. Mike's name was in the papers and I thought this might bring him back, but it did not. Clare wrote from Jocelyn's midlands constituency—a formal expression of regret with a hint that if I was in difficulties she might be able to help, through Jocelyn, of course. I imagined her bitterly, sitting in her office, manipulating people and circumstances; pulling strings, arranging things through the black market—a bribe—a hint of blackmail. I do not know what evidence I had for such a picture, but I never doubted that it was the right one.

I got through to my parents the morning after the accident (the coroner later returned a verdict of 'accidental' death). I could tell from her voice that my mother's asthma was bad. They had retired to the inaccessible farm house perched on a mountainside above Dolgelly because she had been told that she should live high up. It did not seem to have done the asthma much good but it suited them otherwise. My father had never been fond of company and he was happier among the dour Welsh farmers than he had been among the suburban neighbours who had expected to entertain and be entertained. As for my mother, she was content to be where he was content.

She wept down the telephone when I told her my news and insisted that they would come immediately to stay with me. Desperately, I begged them not to, thinking of the chaos on the railways and imagining them struggling with their suitcases from platform to platform or stranded in unheated waiting rooms; thinking, too, of my mother fighting for every breath as she struggled to take the load of household responsibilities from my shoulders and cope with all the attendant circumstances of sudden death; for our leafy and low-lying village suited her less than Wales and emotional disturbance always brought on an attack. Finally I persuaded them to stay where they were, promising that as soon as things were 'a bit more normal' I would bring the children to stay with them.

I thought often of that promise in the following weeks and a great yearning grew in me to be in Wales. 'Away in the lovable west, On the pastoral forehead of Wales'; 'Evening on the olden, the golden sea of Wales, When the first star flickers and the last wave pales . . .' The lines kept running in my head like some oft-repeated charm—a talisman against loss and confusion. 'When it's all over,' I kept telling myself, 'we'll go to Wales.' But, when *what* was all over?

Little by little I forced myself to face the facts of my new situation. Suddenly I had become completely dependent on the State for the means of life for myself and my children. The house, mercifully, was mine now, as the mortgage had been linked to a life insurance policy; but that was all. Most of our meagre savings had gone into buying Mike a partnership and the raging inflation of the last months had taken care of the rest. I tried to sell the car, but the market was already glutted with unwanted vehicles, and I resolved that I would not part with my few pieces of jewellery except in a case of dire necessity. Almost all had been presents from Mike and I loathed the idea of selling them.

There was nothing for it but the long queue at the Social Security office and the endless questions and forms.

I tried to get a job. There was nothing, of course. For the first time I was one of the faceless thousands queuing at the Job Centre and hopelessly tramping the streets. At night I lay awake, physically sick at the thought of the gas bill, the electricity bill, the rates; all those things which I had so happily left to Mike to deal with. I contemplated selling the house, but I knew it would fetch next to nothing in the present state of the market—and, anyway, where would we go? I tried to economize on heating but the weather was still chill and the children were so lost and miserable that I had not the heart to make them suffer cold as well. I fed them as well as I could and told myself that their pallor was only due to shock and the long, cold winter. It was when they begged for the simple luxuries like biscuits and sweets which we had once taken for granted that my pain spilled over into anger and I shouted at them. They did not react but withdrew into silence. Although we had wept together in the first days we were trapped each in our own prison of individual sorrow and I could not come to them.

I suppose it was the result of the election which finally penetrated the deep fog which shrouded me from the outside world, and put me in touch with reality again. No-one could have remained unaware of the atmosphere of suspense and tension, but in the event the result appeared inconclusive. Neither major party was able to command a majority and the National Unity Party members, who included Jocelyn Wentworth, held the balance of power.

After twenty-four hours of confusion a government emerged under the extreme right winger, Martin Emerson. Jocelyn was Home Secretary and other NUP members were prominent in the Cabinet.

That evening we listened to Emerson on the radio. To begin with his speech sounded like many others we had heard over the past few years: the necessity of tightening our belts, facing up to the challenge before us, the dark days ahead, the light at the end of the tunnel . . . then, 'It will be necessary, in this extremity, to sacrifice temporarily—and I emphasize temporarily—some of the democratic rights which we have cherished over the years, even when they obviously militated against national growth and prosperity. Here I have in mind particularly the right to paralyze the country through strike action ...

He ended by declaring that as from midnight troops would take over the running of the power stations and the railways. By dawn we were in the middle of a General Strike. Two days later the Government declared a State of Emergency.

In a strange way the next few days seemed, in our area, like a return to normal. The electricity was on all the time. The shops reopened. The Post Office issued ration books with a promptness which indicated that they must have been prepared under the last Government. With the ration book came an identity card. I know this caused a great deal of anger but, at the time, I could not see any great objection to carrying one. With ever-increasing food shortages and the flourishing black market the ration books were a comfort. It was some time before the stocks became so low that there was not even enough in the shops to supply the ration.

Elsewhere the State of Emergency was not accepted so smoothly. The major unions had refused to capitulate and for a day or two the television news bulletins showed pitched battles in the marshalling yards and at the pit heads and riots in the major cities. After that they became extremely vague about events in England and concentrated mainly on foreign news. The declaration of full scale censorship came soon after and several newspapers abruptly ceased publication.

Shortly after this Jane came in to see me on her way home from school. As we sat over a cup of tea in the kitchen she opened her briefcase and produced three or four sheets of duplicated type-script. These she laid in front of me. The top one was headed 'TROOPS SHOOT DOWN STRIKERS.'

'What's this?' I asked.

'You've heard of "samizdat"?'

I nodded.

'Well,' she jerked her head grimly at the duplicated sheets, 'that's what we're reduced to in this country now. Since the censorship laws a group of journalists have got together to produce an underground newspaper so that people can get the facts about what's really going on. Read it!'

I glanced down the closely typed pages. There were reports from many different areas. The skirmishes between troops and strikers had become pitched battles and on several occasions the soldiers had opened fire, killing a number of people. Leading unionists had been arrested and were being held under the government's emergency powers. Strikers had retaliated with petrol bombs and sabotage, and there were reports of much more sophisticated devices which had been planted in police stations and law courts by a group calling themselves Workers for Freedom, who were claiming support from revolutionary terrorist groups around the world, including the IRA. Another report told of troops being recalled from Germany and Ireland to join the struggle, while yet another told how tanks had encircled a London dock-yard to keep out dockers who wished to prevent troops unloading cargoes from ships there. The editorial claimed that, in spite of the use of troops, the country was slowly grinding to a halt.

I looked up at Jane. 'I didn't realize it was so bad.'

She shrugged. 'That's the whole point, isn't it? People living in relatively quiet areas like this think the rest of the country is the same; while people in the bad areas are encouraged to believe that they are just an isolated pocket of resistance.'

'What are you planning to do?' I asked her.

She shook her head slowly. 'I can't tell you any more at the moment. I just want you to think about it. And when you're thinking, remember this . . .'

She turned over the pages of typescript and showed me another heading. MASSIVE GOVT. 'CARE' CENTRES READY.

I read, 'Reports are coming in from several areas that Local Authorities, on instructions from the government, are planning a massive expansion of places for children in care. Existing centres and homes have been warned that they may have to accept "considerably increased" numbers and in some cases hospitals have been asked to submit plans for accommodating children taken into care. There are also rumours of disused army barracks being made ready to accept children . . .'

I stared at Jane. My mouth had gone dry. 'Why?'

She lifted her shoulders. 'I warned you, months ago. These people may pretend that this government is only a temporary measure to deal with an emergency, but they've no intention of stepping down when the time comes. Emerson, Wentworth—people like that—aren't going to relinquish power now they've got it. They are aiming for a right-wing Totalitarian Government and one thing they need to do if they are going to perpetuate their rule is get hold of the children.'

'But they can't just take them!'

'No, not just like that. But I pointed it out to you! The local authority only has to be convinced that it is "in the child's best interest". With so many people unemployed and homeless do you think they will have trouble finding excuses? And how long will it be before it's decided that the children of dissidents are "at risk"? But there's no need for you to worry at the moment. Be thankful you have a roof over your head!'

A roof, yes! But how long could I go on paying the bills? When Jane had gone I went into the lounge where the boys were watching television with the total passive absorption which had become their defence against disturbing reality. I said nothing, but after a bit Tim came and snuggled against me. I held him close. Simon looked round and I gestured to him to come and sit on my other side, but he gave me a little tight smile and stayed where he was. I knew that it was not myself, in particular, that he was excluding but the world in general; but I would have sold my soul, at that moment, to penetrate his defences.

That night there was another broadcast by the Prime Minister. We were becoming used to the huge bulk of Martin Emerson filling the screen, the small eyes glaring at us out of the heavy-jowled face; but this time his words were more than vague threats and hopeful banalities. Because of continuing unrest and the terrorist activities of a 'handful of left-wing fanatics' it was necessary to impose further restrictions. There was to be a dusk to dawn curfew; gatherings of more than five people were prohibited; anyone wishing to travel more than twenty miles from home must have a permit. In order to help enforce these new regulations and to assist the troops and police in keeping order local units of Civil Militia would be set up, incorporating the TAVR and the existing groups of KBG vigilantes.

'The Government has also felt it necessary,' Emerson's voice was thick and turgid, like cold semolina pudding, 'to take draconian measures to deal with the rising tide of unemployment. The country can no longer afford to pay out vast sums in unemployment benefit to those who are well able to work. We have therefore decided to introduce some direction of labour. Many of our major industries are starved of manpower, either through strikes or for other reasons. From now on, supplementary benefit will no longer be paid to the families of strikers and anyone applying for unemployment benefit will be directed into one of these industries, unless he or she can show positive and irrefutable reasons otherwise. If this entails the movement of workers from one area to another the government will provide cheap rail warrants and accommodation for the workers themselves. We cannot, however, make ourselves responsible for the removal of whole families. I am aware that this redisposition of the labour force may entail, in some cases, particularly in one-parent families, a certain degree of hardship. It is not, however, our intention that the children in these cases should suffer. We are, therefore, taking steps to increase the provision by local authorities of child-care places so that, where there is need, children can be provided with a secure and stable background in which to develop as responsible citizens of the new and greater Britain which we are all striving to build.'

There was a sharp knock at the front door as the broadcast ended. I jumped and felt instantly afraid. Jane would have let herself in through the back door and very few people came visiting in the evening these days. I tried to remember whether the curfew was to have started that night or not until the next.

On the doorstep stood the affable young man who had asked me about squatters and another, older man, smartly dressed, whom I recognized vaguely as a local house-agent. It was this man who spoke first.

'Mrs Fairing? May we come in?'

I experienced a moment of unreasoning panic which brought home to me the full force of the biblical phrase about bowels turning to water.

'What do you want?' I asked.

'Just a few moments of your time. You don't mind, do you? I think you know who we are.'

'I don't know your names,' I gasped, clinging to the last barricades of the old order.

He smiled. 'My name is Harrington, and this is James Piper, but the names are not really important, are they. What matters is that we represent the local committee of the KBG and we should like to talk to you for a few minutes.'

He stepped forward as he spoke, as if quite sure of his right of entry, and preceded me into the lounge. Piper closed the front door behind him and followed. Since they were in it seemed churlish to keep them standing so I asked them to sit down.

'What can I do for you?' The panic was abating now. These were, after all, just ordinary men. In other circumstances, one might have asked them to dinner.

Harrington rested his elbows on the arms of his chair and put his finger tips together. He had a long, narrow face made still longer by receding hair, with deep grooves running from each nostril to the corners of his lips.

'We were sorry to hear about your husband's tragic death, Mrs Fairing.'

I acknowledged the remark without speaking and he went on,

'I believe the verdict was "accidental" death?'

I nodded.

He said, 'Of course, we know that it was not accidental, except in the most trivial and peripheral circumstances.'

'What do you mean?'

'Your husband was killed, Mrs Fairing. He was killed by those striking railmen, just as surely as if one of them had hit him over the head with an iron bar.'

Once again as in so many sleeping and waking nightmares, the picture of the crowded platform with the angry, struggling mob flashed upon my imagination. I got up and turned away from them.

'It seems to me, Mr Harrington, that he was killed just as much by his fellow commuters. Especially by the people who started the fighting.' I looked back at him. 'I heard that it was started by KBG supporters.'

I saw the narrow mouth tighten.

'You mustn't believe rumours, Mrs Fairing. Besides, you can surely sympathize with the anger and frustration of people prevented, through no fault of their own, from going about their lawful business and returning to their wives and families.'

'I don't know about that,' I answered dully. 'I only know they killed my husband.'

I was aware of a glance passing between the two men. Then Harrington said,

'I am sorry to find that your attitude is somewhat—ambivalent. I had hoped that your husband's death would have convinced you of the absolute necessity of supporting those forces which are striving to preserve order in our society.'

Suddenly I was afraid again. I sat down.

'I've always supported law and order. I didn't need convincing by Mike's death—or anything else.'

'Forgive me, Mrs Fairing,' he said smoothly,

'but according to our information you have not always exhibited a very sympathetic attitude towards the present government.'

I stared at him. 'I have never done anything to express my feelings about the present government, one way or the other.'

'Perhaps not since the election,' he agreed. 'But you are aware, of course, that the National Unity Party owes its strength in a very large measure to the KBG movement.'

He paused, looking at me as if requiring a response. I nodded, reluctantly.

'And am I not right in thinking that you encouraged your children to adopt an anti-KBG attitude at school? And that you protested to the Area Education Officer about a talk given at the school by one of our leading members, and attempted to persuade other parents to do the same? Can you still pretend that you have always shown a favourable attitude towards the people who are struggling to get the country back on its feet?'

'I just object to children being involved in politics, that's all.' My voice had become hoarse and strained.

He leaned forward quickly. 'This is not a matter of politics, Mrs Fairing. This is a matter of survival! If we are to survive as a nation, and as individuals, we must forget the party politics of the last decades. We must place ourselves squarely behind the people who see that what this country needs is a strong government and who have the courage to provide it. We need the support and positive effort of every man, woman and child, Mrs Fairing—and, in particular, of people like you. It may sound trite and old-fashioned but we are the backbone of the nation, we of the middle class. We have a sense of responsibility; we have initiative; we have intelligence enough to see where we are heading. The government is relying on people like us. You must do your part. You must throw your weight into the scale of order and sanity!'

He continued to stare at me, his face flushed, a subtle tremor around his lips and nostrils. I said in a low voice,

'What do you expect me to do?'

'First of all, make it clear to everyone that you support us. The local committee holds meetings once a week, on Friday evenings in the village hall. Come to the meetings—and then I am sure we can find you plenty of useful jobs to do.'

'But what about the curfew?' I asked. 'And the regulations forbidding meetings of more than five people?'

He had relaxed again and was smiling. 'Those regulations don't apply to us. We are now part of the new Civil Militia and as such we shall have a good deal of authority in seeing that the new laws are kept, but obviously we are exempt from them ourselves.'

'It's a bit difficult,' I said slowly. 'There are

the children, you see. I can't get out in the evening.'

'Oh come, Mrs Fairing! That's not an insuperable problem. As a matter of fact I've already spoken to your neighbour, Mrs Randall. She and her husband are ardent supporters of ours, you know. She's quite willing to come in and baby-sit for you. And as for the rest—well, after all, you have nothing to do all day, have you, while the children are at school? The country can't afford to support idle people, you know.'

'I've tried to get a job,' I exclaimed. 'I'd like to work, if I could find something.'

He rose and smiled down at me. 'Well, I'm quite sure we can find plenty for you to do. We shall expect to see you at the next meeting, then? Eight o'clock in the village hall. Don't forget.'

The two men moved out into the hall. I followed and as I was about to open the front door Harrington said,

'Oh, and by the way, Mrs Fairing, I shouldn't have too much to do with Jane Grant if I were you. We are aware that her attitude is extremely undesirable and I should not be surprised if she found herself in serious trouble before long. The new regulations forbidding public gatherings and demonstrations are going to be enforced very stringently, I can promise you that. It really is time for everyone to stand up and be

70

counted. Those who are not for us are against us, you know. Goodnight.'

When they had gone I turned on the TV and tried to forget about their visit but I could not rid myself of a sense of unease, as if I was being watched by a critical, unsympathetic eye. I felt cowed and resentful, like I had felt as a child when I had been told off by a teacher. Presently the triviality of the television programmes became irksome rather than comforting and I switched off in order to concentrate on sorting out my feelings. Out of a few moments' thought came a sudden burst of anger. What right had those men to intrude on my life and make me feel afraid? Soberly I reminded myself that I must expect this, and much worse, if events continued in their present direction; and out of that thought came a decision.

The next day I telephoned Jane at school and asked her to call on her way home. She came, and I told her about the previous evening.

'I suppose it's the classic case of the worm turning,' I said, 'but I'm not going to have my life run by men like Harrington. So I'll do what I can. But I'm not brave, Jane, and the boys come before anything. I'd better warn you now. Don't tell me anything secret. I couldn't promise to keep it if—well, if there was any trouble. And I won't do anything involving violence.'

I looked at her, seated at my kitchen table with her feet thrust out and her hands deep in the pockets of her shabby cardigan. She tilted her chair and asked,

'What's that supposed to mean?'

'What I said. There's one thing I want to be sure of, Jane. You're not anything to do with Workers for Freedom, are you?'

She made a small sound of exasperation. 'Can you really see me getting involved with terrorists? Have you ever known me involved with violent groups of any sort?'

I shook my head.

'Well, then!' She relaxed and gave me a grin. 'Never mind. Point taken. Now listen. I'm not going to tell you any more than I have to, for the reasons you've just given me. Not that there's very much I could tell you, because I don't know any more than I have to, either. Oddly enough, you're not the only person to feel that way. All you need to know is that there are people all over the country who are determined not to sit back and accept what has happened. So ultimately there are going to be protests and demonstrations on a massive scale and no-one knows yet how the Government will react to that. Ultimately it may come to an armed confrontation but only in the last resort. What matters is to mobilize people all over the country at the same moment. We have to be sure that we don't go off at half-cock. Isolated, small-scale demonstrations just get people arrested and produce nothing. With the clamp down on news no-one outside the immediate area knows that anything has happened. We must co-ordinate with all the other groups who are trying to resist, especially with the strikers— and we must let people know what is happening in other areas. Our immediate aim is to collect information about what is going on round here and to pass that on to the others.'

'Is there some sort of national organization?' I asked.

Jane shook her head. 'Not yet. Only various groups like us all over the place, under dozens of different banners. That's the point. We have to get an organization going.'

I sat down opposite her, feeling suddenly calm and efficient—like I felt when Timmy cut his leg so badly and I knew I had to stop the bleeding.

'Where do I come in?'

'You can be very useful. Obviously Harrington and Co think that you can be brow-beaten into supporting them. No doubt Clare told them that you were political putty that just needed a firm hand to mould it.' She grinned at me and I grinned back, feeling closer to her than I had for years. 'Pretend to go along with them. Go to the meetings, and keep me informed about what goes on.'

I considered the prospect. My common-sense reminded me that when the rush of

73

adrenalin subsided the high-powered, super cool efficiency would collapse into quivering exhaustion. But it was a relief for once to do as well as to suffer.

'What do you want to know?'

She shrugged. 'Anything. What are they up to? I know they're supposed to be a sort of watch-dog, making sure that everyone toes the line and gets on with the job. But do they do anything more than watch? And who, particularly, are they watching? O.K.?'

'O.K. I'll do my best.'

'Don't, for God's sake, try and take notes or anything, will you?'

It was my turn to look exasperated. 'Give me some credit! Anyway, I happen to have something very close to total recall, remember?'

'After all the long, rambling tales I've had to listen to?' said Jane. 'I should forget!'

I was right about the collapse of resolve. By Friday night I was full of sick foreboding and it took Molly Randall's air of do-gooding condescension when she came to baby-sit to brace me for the effort of attending the meeting. There were about two hundred people in the village hall. Many of the faces were vaguely familiar. I had never been a joiner and did not know who were the leading lights in the various local organizations but there were a number of people I knew casually and by chatting to them I began to pick up

74

names and functions—local councillors; committee members of the W.I.; a Guide Commissioner; the Chairman of the Residents Association; members of the Rotary Club and the Chamber of Commerce. The village establishment was there in force. 'How beastly the bourgeois is' D. H. Lawrence said once. It was true that night. It was like a kind of Walpurgisnacht in which all the long-supressed instinctual urges of the middle-class were allowed to run wild. All the old prejudices and class-hatreds were taken out and given an airing; all the half-forgotten fears and the old bogeys were re-examined and pronounced well-founded. The unions, the communists, the blacks, students, left-wing social workers and long-haired teachers were lined up like Aunt Sallies and duly shot down in a succession of speeches. The climax came when Harrington, who was chairing the meeting, said,

'Now, ladies and gentlemen, the time has come when we ask all of you for your co-operation in ensuring that everyone in our community is pulling his weight and doing his—or her—utmost towards National Recovery. If there is anyone whom you know is not doing this, this is the moment for you to tell us about it.'

That was when the denunciations started. In tones of smug self-satisfaction and sincere moral indignation the local worthies pursued

75

long-standing, previously hidden feuds and irritations. The first to speak was a square-fared, harsh-voiced woman whom I had often noticed shouting at her brood of children when she collected them from school. The object of her complaint was a local doctor, as it happened our family G.P. He was, I knew, inclined to be brusque with those whose problems arose largely from their own incompetence but I had found him able and sympathetic when real need arose. Now the harsh voice accused him of giving medical certificates to men who were really on strike. Harrington nodded and murmured to a companion, who made a note.

The second denunciation concerned a local builder who had, it appeared, closed down his yard rather than employ black-leg labour. Once again Harrington and his friend conferred and a note was made. As he spoke Harrington glanced towards the back of the hall. There had been a good deal of noise from this quarter during the meeting in the form of vociferous support for various speakers and, lately, threatening murmurs against those accused. I glanced round and saw that it emanated from a group which seemed to assort oddly with the rest of the meeting, consisting as it did of young men and girls, teenagers many of them, with short cropped hair and red, white and blue KBG T-shirts. Not the type, I thought, who would normally involve themselves in local politics.

The meeting was almost over, but before I left I was buttonholed by Harrington's wife and had to promise to help out with typing and other clerical jobs. Her manner was effusively charming—she might have been asking me to help with the PTA social. There was no alternative but to agree.

On Sunday morning I took the boys for a walk. For the first time since the previous autumn there was some warmth in the sun. The hazel trees on the common were furred with yellow catkins and the first crocuses showed in the gardens we passed. Simon and Tim capered about, shouting and chasing each other, breaking off now and then to climb trees or fish for frog-spawn. It was the first time I had seen them happy since Mike's death.

On the way home we happened to pass the yard of the builder who had been denounced on Friday evening. My nostrils caught the tang of burnt wood before we rounded the corner. Above the boundary wall we could see the blackened girders which were all that remained of the buildings inside and smoke still rising in wisps and spirals on the quiet air. On the wall someone had painted the words—COMMUNIST SYMPATHISER— YOU HAVE BEEN WARNED!

When we reached home I telephoned my doctor. His wife offered to give me the number of another GP. Her husband could see nobody at present. His surgery had been burnt to the ground the night before.

When Jane arrived the following evening I could scarcely wait for her to get through the door before I began pouring out the whole story. She listened, sitting on the edge of the kitchen table while I paced around, distractedly putting out the tea cups as I talked. When I had finished she nodded grimly and said,

'And in a few days when the organization gets going for these Civil Militia units those people are going to have guns in their hands.'

The next Friday night followed the same pattern as the previous one. There was only one denunciation which appeared to me to be taken seriously by the men on the platform. A woman complained that a local grocer was selling his stock on the black market. I had shopped there for years and had seen the man only the day before looking worn and anxious as he struggled to make the inadequate supplies go round. No-one was getting their full ration but I was convinced it was not his fault. The next morning I passed the information on to Jane. On Monday she told me that the shop had been broken into by 'looters' on Saturday night but, forewarned, the grocer had moved his stock to a secret place. On Monday, in spite of broken windows and smashed fittings, it was business as usual.

After Jane had left I reflected soberly that the KBG looters must have realized that the shop-keeper had been warned and wondered how long it would be before they began to suspect the source of the information. I began to feel that I would be wise not to report the next accusations—if my conscience would let me keep silent. In the event, I had other things to think about by the following weekend.

On Thursday Jane came in unexpectedly and I could see that she was excited.

'Nell, listen!' She dropped into a chair and fixed me with her eyes. 'I want you to do something for me. Could you have my kids to stay on Friday night and look after them on Saturday?'

'Yes, of course I will,' I answered automatically. I had done it before, often enough. But now I felt a sudden jerk of apprehension in my stomach. 'Why?'

'I wouldn't be telling you this if you hadn't proved yourself in the last week or two,' she began. In times of excitement Jane's inner conviction of superior moral toughness came to the surface. I was used to this and still grateful, as in childhood, for her qualified approval. 'You remember I told you we were planning for a concerted effort, a really big demonstration to make people realize that there is still massive opposition to Emerson and his government. Well, it's planned for Saturday.'

'Where?'

'Windsor.'

'Why on earth Windsor?' I exclaimed.

'Oh, use your head, Nell! Where are the Royal Family at the moment?'

'I haven't any idea.'

'No, I'm not surprised. Haven't you noticed that since Emerson went to the palace immediately after the election there has been virtually no mention of the Queen or any other member of the Royal Family, in any of the media? Our information is that they are at Windsor—all of them. The Prince of Wales has been recalled and the whole family have been cooped up at Windsor ever since Emerson took over.'

'You don't mean he's keeping them prisoners there, do you?' I stared at her, wondering if she and her associates were as sane as I had taken them to be.

'Nobody knows for sure what's going on,' she replied. 'The rumour is that they are opposed to Emerson and one of them—you can guess who—wanted to speak out against him. If that's true then he obviously couldn't risk having them going about in public. Of course, the official story is that they are staying at Windsor for their own safety until the State of Emergency is over. But if there's any truth in the rumours we may have found the rallying point we want. That's why Windsor has been chosen.'

'But you'll never get anywhere near them.'

'No, of course not. But they are bound to know we are there. And what is more important, the soldiers on duty there will know. That's the key, Nell. Emerson can only keep control as long as the army backs him. If the army can be convinced that he is trying to destroy the constitution and even keep the Queen a prisoner that should finish him. We've heard rumours of small scale mutinies, here and there, in units which have been ordered to fire on demonstrators, but we have to get at the top brass. What we need is a focus, Nell! Windsor and the Royal Family could provide it.'

'How are you going to get there?' I asked. 'What about the twenty mile limit?'

'We're going to travel by night. That's why I want you to have the children on Friday evening.' She leaned forward, her eyes bright and her usually sallow face flushed with excitement. 'I know it's risky, with the curfew and everything, but we're banking on the fact that the army and the police are too over-stretched to cover every lane and minor road. Someone I know has managed to get hold of a tank-full of petrol. We hope to get there just before dawn and just slip into the town. The authorities shouldn't know that anything is happening until they suddenly find hundreds of people massed outside the castle.'

'But Jane,' I protested. 'They can't miss

hundreds of people. As soon as there are more than five they can arrest you.'

'They can't arrest hundreds,' she pointed out reasonably. 'The first few, perhaps. That's just a risk we have to take.' Her face grew more sober. 'I know there are all sorts of problems and dangers, Nell; but if we don't get some sort of united effort going soon Emerson will have a strangle hold on the whole country. Look, you'll have to go to the meeting as usual. I'll bring the kids round afterwards. If anybody asks questions you can tell them I've gone off for a dirty weekend.'

'And what am I supposed to do if you get yourself arrested?'

We met each other's eyes across the table. I thought of Jane's three children; Edward and Bill, both a year or so older than my boys, and little Elizabeth who had only just started school.

Jane said, 'There are people who would help—with money and things. Would you try to cope?'

I nodded and said flatly, 'Yes, I'll cope.' That was what life came down to, these days.

All through Saturday I waited for news, trying to hide my anxiety from the children who were happy and excited all together. It was not until early evening that the radio carried a report that a number of people had been arrested under the emergency regulations after attempting to stage a demonstration outside Windsor Castle.

Just after dark came a hasty, brief knocking on the door. An unknown young man stood outside. Instinctively, as if I had been bred to conspiracy, I stepped back and let him in, closing the door behind him. The children were in the lounge, noisily playing Monopoly, except for the little girl who was already in bed.

The man said, 'You're Nell Fairing?' I nodded and he went on, 'You don't know me. I teach at the same school as Jane Grant. My name's Nick Saunders.'

I asked tensely, 'Did you go with her today?'

'Yes, that's why I'm here.' He stopped suddenly and looked at me unhappily. 'I had to come and tell you.'

'Has Jane been arrested?' I spoke with sudden harshness, gripping the edge of the table.

'Yes.'

'Oh God!' I sat down quickly and put my hands over my face. For a moment I felt as if my whole personality was about to break up under the ever-increasing strain.

He said, 'I'm sorry. You've got her kids, I know. I'll help, if I can.'

Even at the moment of greatest stress there is no merciful oblivion for most of us, no abrogation of responsibility in fainting or hysteria. The moment has to be faced and passed. I raised my head.

'And it was all a flop! All this for nothing!'

'No!' He sat down quickly, opposite me. 'No! What gave you that idea? It was fantastic. You should have seen it.'

'Tell me about it.' I gripped my hands together and stared at him.

He leaned on the table so that our faces were only a foot or two apart.

'We got there without any trouble. All the back lanes were quite open, not a soldier in sight. A lot of people from the north had problems because they had to cross the Thames and all the bridges were guarded, but some of them commandeered boats and rowed across in the dark and one big group who had come all the way from Birmingham sandbagged the sentries at one bridge and opened it up for a whole lot of others. Everyone came into the town on foot, in twos and threes as we'd been told and as soon as we were in the town we found places to hide out until there were other people around. Then we made our way towards the castle gates. That was the tricky bit. There were police on duty all round, keeping people moving, and of course we couldn't tell which were our people and which weren't. We had to walk up and down the hill a couple of times until the deadline arrived. Then someone suddenly produced a banner saying FREEDOM UNDER THE QUEEN and immediately there was a great roar and hundreds of people rushed towards the castle gates. They were shut, of course. The castle hasn't been open to the public since the emergency started. Everyone was shouting "Down with the Dictators!" and "Give us back our Constitution!" and "Emerson Out!" and "We want the Queen!" The police couldn't do anything against that many and you could see that the sentries inside the gates didn't know what to do. They stood there at attention, like dummies, but you could see their eyes swivelling from side to side. That was when Jane started. We were right at the front of the crowd, quite close to one of them. She got hold of the bars and started shouting to him, telling him that his loyalty should be to the British Constitution and to the Queen, not to a government which was trying to set up a dictatorship, and so on. By that time the rest of the guard had turned out and she started haranguing them, too. A sergeant spotted her and pointed her out to the police. They'd been reinforced, too, by then, but they couldn't fight their way through the crowd to get at her. Then the troops proper arrived, in armoured cars with water cannon and so on. We hung on as long as we could but no crowd can hold together against water cannon. Then we saw them putting on gas masks. Well, we knew what that meant. It was the tear gas that really broke it all up. You can't see or breathe properly. I'd seen it on telly, of course, in

Ireland and in Paris in '68. I'd never realized how ghastly it is. Six months ago I couldn't have imagined it being used here, could you? Of course, as soon as the crowd broke up the police charged in. They'd had plenty of opportunity to pick out what looked like the ring-leaders. They got Jane and several others. There wasn't anything we could do except run for it and hope to get out of the town before they organized a police cordon. We took a risk on driving back in daylight. We nearly ran into a road block in Chobham but there are plenty of back lanes, thank heaven.' He came to a stop, like a clockwork toy running down and sat staring at me.

I said automatically, 'You must be hungry.'

He made the routine protests, but ate the bread and dripping which I put in front of him.

'What will happen to Jane?' I asked.

He shrugged. 'She'll be detained under the emergency powers, I suppose.'

'That means no trial?'

'That's right.'

'So we shan't know how long . . .'

'Until we get this Government out,' he said with sudden vehemence, and added more gently, 'It can't be long.'

'Is there any chance of finding out where she is and being able to visit her?'

He shook his head. 'I doubt it. We can try.'

There was a pause. He continued,

'What will you do—about the children?'

86

I sat down heavily. 'I promised her I'd look after them. She said other people would help—with money and things.'

He nodded quickly. 'Leave that to me. I'll organize that end of it. What about their ration books?'

'I suppose Jane must have them at Well Cottage.'

'Right.' His tone was businesslike now. 'I'll get hold of them tonight and let you have them tomorrow. And I'll bring some of their clothes and things. Is there anything else I can do right now?'

He looked dead tired already. I said,

'No. Don't worry. I can manage.'

Jane had told the children that she would be away for the whole weekend, so they were not expecting her back that night. The next morning I called them all to me. I had always believed that children had a right to the truth though that day I would have given much for the refuge of a comfortable lie. When I told them about Jane's arrest there was a moment of stunned silence. Then Bill, the younger said tremulously,

'They can't put Mummy in prison. What about us?'

'You'll have to stay with us for a bit longer, Bill,' I said. 'Don't worry. I'll look after you. The important thing for you to remember is that your mother hasn't done anything wrong. It's only because the whole country is in such a bad state that all this has happened. When it gets sorted out she'll be able to come home again.'

'When will that be?' he asked.

I put my arm round him. Why did I find it so awkward to cuddle other people's children? 'I don't know, love. Perhaps it won't be long.'

My boys had listened in silence when I broke the news to the others. Later they found me in the kitchen. Simon said,

'You won't do anything to get arrested, will you Mum?'

I looked at them, standing side by side, pale and serious.

'Don't you think Edward and Bill's Mum was right, then, to stand up for what she believes in?'

They came and stood close to me.

'I suppose so . . .' Simon said slowly. 'But . . .'

Timmy threw his arms round me suddenly. 'We don't want you to go to prison, Mummy!'

I held them both to me. 'I'm not going to do anything that might take me away from you, I promise!' I met Simon's eyes. 'Not if I can help it,' I added, almost under my breath.

The children were getting ready for bed when the knock came. It was Harrington with a policeman and a woman in civilian clothes. Harrington said,

'Mrs Fairing, I understand that you have the children of Mrs Jane Grant in your care.'

I swallowed. 'Yes, they are staying with me for the weekend. Why?'

'May we come in, please?'

They went into the lounge. Upstairs, I could hear the children's voices, subdued for once to a low murmur.

Harrington faced me. 'Are you aware that Jane Grant was arrested yesterday?'

I almost admitted it. The habit of deception was not yet established. Instead I said,

'Arrested?'

'Yes.'

'What for?'

He looked at me narrowly. 'For taking part in an illegal demonstration and attempting to incite members of Her Majesty's forces to mutiny.'

I stared back at him. I had control of myself now. This man had no authority. He was just a jumped up house-agent who fancied himself as a petty tyrant.

'Jane?' I said, in tones of amazement.

'I've warned you before about your friend's dangerous views,' he said tersely. 'May I ask why the children are here? What excuse did she give for leaving them? Or were you aware of her intentions?'

'No, of course not.' Did that sound too vehement? 'She would hardly tell me something like that. She knows I don't want to be involved. She wanted to spend the weekend with a friend. You understand, being

89

divorced—and with the children; sometimes she needed to get away. I've often looked after the children for her.'

He raised his eyebrows with an expression of distaste. 'Really? Well, it may interest you to know that this time she somehow got herself to Windsor, where she took part in a left-wing demonstration. As I told you, she is now under arrest. That being so, and there being no other legal guardian, we have arranged for the children to be taken into care. Miss Stephens here will take them as soon as they can be got ready.'

For a moment I could think of nothing to say. Then I mumbled foolishly,

'But they're getting ready for bed.'

'Then you had better stop them before they go any further and tell them to get dressed again,' Harrington said.

I pulled myself together. 'There's no need for you to take them. I promised—I mean, I'll take care of them.'

'Promised, Mrs Fairing?' The grooves beside his mouth deepened as his lips tightened.

'If anything ever happened—years ago, I promised—when Jane got her divorce.'

'Well, I am afraid you are no longer in a position to carry out that promise, are you? Besides, in giving the children into care you will be doing the best thing possible for them. Surely that is keeping your promise?'

'No!' I said, desperation growing in me. 'No, you can't take them. They know me. It's cruel to take them away.'

'Nonsense, Mrs Fairing!' His voice was growing sharp and the Stephens woman was shifting her handbag restlessly. She was quite a young woman but her thickset body and sturdy legs in the flat-heeled shoes seemed to be the visible expression of deaf authority and her face was impassive. Harrington went on, 'We really haven't time for all this sentimentality. Children are very adaptable. Their mother must have been fully aware of the implications of her actions. They will be properly cared for, away from subversive influences. Miss Stephens, go up and fetch the Grant children down, please.'

'No!' I said. 'I'll go—I'll explain to them . . .'

Miss Stephens was already moving towards the door. I made to intercept her but Harrington said sharply, 'Mrs Fairing!' and the policeman took a step towards me. I watched the other woman leave the room and then turned on Harrington,

'Why couldn't you leave them with me? I could have cared for them.'

'Really, Mrs Fairing?' He asked smoothly. 'What about food? We have rationing remember?'

'I—I would have got their ration books. They must be at the cottage somewhere.'

He reached into his breast pocket and drew

91

out three ration books.

'We caught a young man who had broken into the cottage this morning. He was about to remove these, together with some of the children's clothes. He appears to have been one of Jane Grant's associates. It took us sometime to persuade him to tell us where the children were. Of course, I should have thought of you.' He seated himself, letting the words hang in the air as he returned the ration books to his pocket. I thought of Nick Saunders' haggard, eager face as he described the demonstration and his quiet determination. How had they 'persuaded' him? Harrington went on. 'Mrs Fairing, I have warned you more than once about Jane Grant. I am prepared to believe that you were unaware of her real purpose this weekend but you must realize that your own position is now somewhat—shall we say precarious? I don't know, of course, what your financial circumstances are, but I imagine that you must be more or less dependent on social security since your husband's death. The time is coming when only those who can show that they are whole-heartedly behind the government will receive such benefits. If there was ever any doubt in your case—it might become necessary to take your children into care also.'

I turned my back on him and grasped the back of a chair. All my muscles had gone slack and I was finding it hard to breathe properly. Outside the room there was a commotion of voices and footsteps and Edward burst into the room.

'Auntie Nell—this woman says she's come to take us away!'

Miss Stephens came in, holding little Elizabeth tightly by the hand. The child was crying and trying to pull away. Bill followed, shouting,

'Let her go! Let her go!'

Harrington overrode the noise.

'Be quiet, all of you, and listen to me! Your mother is in prison because she broke the law; but that does not mean that we wish you to be punished too. You are going to be well looked after, with enough to eat and plenty of other boys and girls to play with. There are many children who do not have either food or friends, so you are fortunate. There is no point in arguing. If you stayed here Mrs Fairing would not be able to feed you all. So go along with Miss Stephens and behave sensibly. Take them out to the car, Miss Stephens.'

The woman turned away, catching Bill's arm with her free hand. He struggled. Edward made a movement of appeal in my direction.

'But, Auntie Nell, you said . . .'

I shook my head, the tears streaming down my face. 'There's nothing I can do, Edward. Nothing!'

He looked at me for a long moment and

then slowly turned away. Bill ceased to struggle and Miss Stephens made her way purposefully towards the door. The constable laid a hand on Edward's shoulder and propelled him after her. In silence they left the house. In the doorway Harrington turned.

'Remember, Mrs Fairing. Those who do not support the government cannot expect to be supported by it. Goodnight.'

As the door closed I could hear Elizabeth screaming 'I want my Mummy! I want my Mummy!' A car started, doors banged, and the sound of the engine died away.

Simon and Tim were huddled together on the stairs. As I turned from the door they rushed down and flung themselves upon me. It took me a long time to convince them that they were not going to be taken away also. At length I got them to bed and sat with them until they were asleep. Then, sitting in the darkness, I made my plans.

The car had a tank full of petrol. I had not used it since the emergency began. That would take us how far? 240 miles. We could get to Dolgelly on that. There were the road-blocks, of course, but Jane and her friends had managed to avoid them. If I kept to the back lanes it would take longer, but we could still reach Wales in a day. And once there, deep in the mountains, surely no-one would bother to track us down.

My first impulse was to start at once but I

reflected that the sound of a car driving off in the middle of the night would be certain to alert the neighbours. Anyway, there was the curfew to consider. If I left just before nine tomorrow I could always say, if challenged, that I was taking the children to school.

I got up and fetched two suitcases. Swiftly I packed as many clothes as I could take for the three of us. Then I filled two cardboard boxes with all the food I could lay my hands on and crept out to load it all into the car under cover of darkness. Then I crawled into bed and lay, tense and wakeful, waiting for morning. My conscience troubled me. I felt that I should stay and try to find out where Jane's children were and visit them; try to contact Jane; keep them in touch with each other. But I remembered Harrington's warnings and my own children's faces, and thought of the quiet of the mountains; and the voice of argument died. This was where friendship and social responsibility ended. From now on it was me and mine.

CHAPTER FOUR

CENTRIFUGE

By first light I was up, sorting through maps and planning our route. I remembered that

Nick Saunders had mentioned road blocks. But where—and how frequent were they? Nick had said that all the bridges over the Thames were guarded. I must keep south of the river then, until it bent northwards at Reading. West of Oxford it might be easier to cross. Where else would I find roadblocks? The motorways appeared formidable barriers on the map; but I remembered the many lanes and farm tracks which crossed them. Surely they could not all be guarded. Towns, of course, must be avoided if possible; but how large a centre of population dare I risk passing through? Would every village present a hazard? I had no idea. Perhaps Jane and Nick had been dramatizing. After all, Nick had driven back from Windsor without being stopped. Suppose I was stopped? Was it an offence to attempt to travel beyond the twenty-mile limit, or would I simply be turned back and told to go home?

I pulled myself together and shuffled the maps into a pile. There was no point in guessing. I must simply be prepared for each eventuality as it arose. Whatever the consequences I was determined not to stay where I was any longer.

I woke the children and prepared breakfast, using up the last of my egg ration in a prodigal omelette. Over the food I told Simon and Tim what we were going to do. Their eyes grew wide.

'You mean we're not going to school?' asked Tim.

'No, I'm afraid you'll have to miss a bit of school. You'll catch it up later.' My heart gave a lurch. When would they be able to go back to school? Could I send them in Dolgelly?

'Won't they mind—at school, I mean?' Simon asked. He was always the more cautious of the two, and more far-seeing.

'We aren't going to tell them, Simon,' I said quietly. 'Now listen. No, listen, Tim!' He had started a sing-song "We're not going to school. We're not going to school!" This is difficult for you to understand, I know, but just believe me. You know things aren't, well, normal, at the moment and we can't do a lot of things we used to be able to do. I'm afraid if people knew we were going to Granny and Grandad's they might try to stop us, so we're not going to tell anyone. No one at all. Do you understand?'

'Why?' said Simon. 'Why would they want to stop us?'

I did my best to explain. After some thought he said,

'We shall be breaking the law then, shan't we.'

'Just this one, particular law.'

'It's a stupid law, anyway,' said Tim. 'You don't have to obey stupid laws, do you Mummy?'

I felt their eyes on me and said, 'Come on.

Let's get these dishes cleared away.'

Neither of them pursued the subject, but I caught Simon's gaze once or twice and flinched inwardly.

We cleared up and finished packing. I made the boys tidy their room. I even made the beds, as if we should be back in a day or two. I looked into the room we had given Alan and Clare. Alan's suits still hung in the wardrobe. As I opened the door they emitted a faint but powerful male smell which made me feel suddenly weak in the pit of my stomach. I had got Jane to dispose of all Mike's clothes soon after his death because I could not bear the lingering odour which clung to them. It surprised me that Alan's smell should have such a strong effect on me.

I wondered what would happen if he came back after we had gone and contemplated leaving a note for him. Then I remembered how Harrington and his men had searched Jane's cottage. I would leave no clues for them. In a sudden rush I hunted out all the old letters I could find from my parents and made a bonfire with them in the garden.

I turned off the gas and the water and unplugged the television. Then I locked the back door and took a last look round. The boys were waiting in the hall. I smiled at them.

'Come on! It's like going off for a holiday, isn't it! By tonight we shall be at Granny's.'

I was trembling as I backed the car out of

the drive, almost expecting Harrington or one of his men to appear and demand to know where I was going. I deliberately set off as if I was taking the boys to school and then doubled back, resolutely avoiding looking at anyone passing me on the pavement, as if by so doing I could render myself invisible. It was not until we were well away from the village that I began to relax.

For the first part of the journey I needed no maps. Here the main roads ran west and south from London. Our route crossed them in a series of dog's legs, tending always north-west through pastureland on into the heaths and pine woods of Berkshire. At a junction with the A30 we had to wait while a long convoy of army trucks and tanks rumbled past, heading towards London. The boys bounced up and down on the back seat with delighted exclamations. I gripped the steering wheel and felt my heart beating.

There were few cars on the roads. As long as we were in the country lanes this did not worry me but when we were forced for a while to follow a larger road the absence of traffic made me feel uneasily conspicuous. Then, just outside Bracknell, I came up behind a queue of vehicles on a bend. I knew there was a roundabout ahead. Perhaps we were just waiting for another convoy to pass—or perhaps not. Without hesitating I swung the wheel and turned the car onto the other carriage way. It took me some time to find a way to by-pass that section of road, but I managed it in the end.

I edged south of Wokingham and began to follow the line of the M4 planning to get to the west of Reading before I crossed it and headed north. There was a good deal of helicopter activity above us and once one dropped down to within a few hundred feet and appeared to be inspecting us. Then I saw ahead of me a section of the motorway on a raised embankment. Along it at intervals the hunched outlines of tanks stood against the sky, their gun turrets swivelled to point north. I took the next turning and made a wide sweep before approaching the motorway again further west. I chose a narrow lane which, according to the map, passed under the motorway. The fields were empty on either side and the only house we passed appeared to be deserted. Then three men stepped out from behind a barn and barred my way.

They were in civilian dress—jeans and anoraks. One stepped forward and leaned down to look in through my window. Hesitantly I wound it down.

'What do you want?'

'We was wondering where you was headed for,' he said, quite pleasantly but looking, I thought, puzzled.

I had my story ready.

'I'm going to visit a friend near Oxford.'

'Well, you won't get there,' he said flatly.

'Why not?' I asked.

He frowned at me. The other two had come closer and I saw them exchange glances. One of them was quite young, around twenty perhaps. He came and leaned down to me also.

'Have you come far? It was an educated voice, different from the first man's, with a slight west-country burr.

'Not very,' I said, 'Look, what is all this?'

In the back of the car the boys squirmed uneasily. I had impressed on them that if we were stopped they must say nothing. Once again the men exchanged glances and then the younger one said,

'If you lived around here you wouldn't need to ask. You won't get to Oxford because the whole countryside between here and there is saturated with army units and every road is blocked.'

'But why?' I asked helplessly.

The two men straightened up and conferred in undertones. Then the first one bent again and said,

'Look, is it really important—for you to get through to this friend? Because if it isn't the best thing you can do is turn round and go home.'

'It is important,' I said earnestly. 'Really it is.'

'All right, then,' he said heavily. 'But I can't

let you go on on your own. The best thing I can do for you is send you through to our headquarters and see what they say about it. If they think you might have a chance—well, that's up to them.'

I tried to ask 'What headquarters?' but he went on,

'Jim'll come with you. You'd best let him drive. He knows the roads better and which areas to avoid.'

The younger man opened the car door and smiled in a friendly manner.

'Would you mind moving over? Don't worry. You'll be perfectly safe with us.'

Helplessly, unsure whether to be encouraged or afraid, I eased myself into the passenger seat and Jim took my place. He spoke a few words more with his companions, then started the engine and drove on down the lane.

'Where are we going?' I asked.

'Into the city,' he replied.

I felt panic grab at my stomach. 'But I don't want to go into the city.'

'Look,' he said, 'you don't understand the situation. You're not just out for a country drive, you know. You're in a war zone.'

'But why?' I cried. 'You're right. I don't understand. What is going on?'

'Do you mean to say it's all quiet where you come from?' He glanced swiftly at me, frowning.

'Well, pretty quiet, yes. I mean—not like this with tanks all over the place and everything.'

He sighed. 'Looks as if we are on our own then. Somehow I thought the rest of the country would be doing the same as us.'

'What are you doing?' I persisted.

He did not answer at once. There were houses ahead and he made a sharp turn into a side street, peering ahead of him with acute concentration. Then he relaxed a little and said,

'When the General Strike was called all the workers in Reading came out and started demonstrations and marches. We joined them—I'm a student, you see, at the University. To begin with it was all fairly good tempered—well, as much as you could expect a political demonstration to be. The police couldn't do much, there were too many of us. It went on for several days. We occupied University buildings and factories, burnt our identity cards, refused to respect the curfew. Then they sent the troops in. I suppose their big mistake was that they didn't send quite enough. After that the feeling changed. It became a battle. They hit us with tear gas and water cannon, and then they started using rubber bullets. We built barricades and attacked public buildings. It was like Paris in '68.' He broke off with a shrug and a half laugh. 'I never thought of myself as a militant.

Agriculture's my subject.'

'If it comes to that, I've never thought of myself as a—fugitive,' I said. 'But I'm beginning to feel like one. Is it still going on?'

He looked grim. 'It can't go on much longer. To begin with we felt we were getting on top. We made contact with Oxford and the same thing was going on there. We thought it must be the same over the whole country. People said the government couldn't last more than a few days. By then, of course, the "leaders" had appeared. We were getting organized.'

'What sort of leaders?' I asked. I was beginning to feel at ease with this quietly spoken young man whose matter-of-fact approach was tinged with irony.

Once again he lifted his shoulders slightly.

'The people who make a career out of violence and unrest. I don't know where they come from. You'll see.'

We were entering the outskirts of the city, keeping to the side-roads with their long, drab-looking terraces. The roads were almost deserted and the few people we saw moved furtively, keeping close to the buildings. I began to see the evidence of what had happened in the last weeks. Windows were smashed, street furniture twisted and broken, burnt out cars stood at crazy angles across the road, forcing Jim to slow to a crawl. Then we came to a barricade of derelict vehicles and bits of furniture. Jim stopped the car and went forward to confer with the group of men standing by it. Simon leaned over to me and hissed urgently,

'Where are we going, Mum?'

I tried to smile reassuringly. 'We've got to see some people, that's all. It'll be all right.'

'What people . . .?' he began, but I hushed him quickly. Now that the car was stationary I was becoming aware of a distant noise, a constant roar which fluctuated in volume but never died away—the sound of many hundreds of voices.

Jim came back. 'We'll have to try a different route. There's a battle going on up ahead.'

He reversed the car and set off again through a warren of small streets.

I said, 'Why did you say it couldn't last much longer?'

'You saw the tanks,' he replied briefly. 'About three or four days ago we suddenly heard that they were drafting in hundreds more troops. Since then we've been losing ground steadily. We've occupied the Buttes— the big new shopping precinct—it'll take them a good while to drive us out of there, unless they decide to shell the place, but they are bound to win in the end. They say Oxford has fallen already. That's why we couldn't let you go on.'

We turned into a larger road, empty except for a burnt out double-decker bus. I could hear the crowd noise above the sound of the engine now. Suddenly half a dozen running figures burst out from a side street ahead of us and in a few seconds the junction was filled with a surging mass of people. Jim braked sharply and then swung the car around. The bus restricted his area of manoeuvre and by the time he had turned the crowd had reached us and we were surrounded by running figures. There were men of all ages and a sprinkling of girls; some were dressed in working clothes, some in trendy denim, some in motor-bike leathers. Many wore crash helmets or the sort of tin hats issued to building workers and had scarves wrapped about their faces. The first few ran on past us, obviously intent on losing themselves in the streets ahead, but the next comers saw a rallying point in the derelict bus. The crowd checked and milled around us. Some banged on the roof of the car and shouted. A dozen or more laid hold of the car and began to rock it, clearly intending to add it to the partial barricade formed by the bus. Tim was screaming in the back seat.

Jim wound down his window and yelled at the people nearest him. His words were lost in the roar but I heard him say 'The Irishman'. A man bent to listen to him, peered at us and then straightened up to shout at his companions. More faces stared in at us and the car ceased to rock. Through a gap in the crowd round us I caught a glimpse of the road junction from which they had appeared. I could see three armoured vehicles advancing inexorably into the mass, water cannon sweeping the way ahead of them. Between them foot soldiers held a steady line, bayonets fixed.

The car engine revved and we jerked forward. The crowd was parting to let us through. Slowly we inched ahead towards the clearer road. From in front of us a party of perhaps twenty young men came charging down in a disciplined formation to join the battle now raging around the bus. They carried metal shields and at least some of them, I saw with a shock which only registered later, were armed with rifles.

We were almost clear of the crowd when the explosion came, jolting us all in our seats and making me feel as though I had been struck violently in the middle of the chest. Jim braked violently and we all twisted in our seats to look behind us. The far end of the street was momentarily hidden by dense smoke which revealed as it cleared the twisted remains of one of the armoured vehicles. There was a crescendo of yells and screams as the crowd of demonstrators swept forward again, taking advantage of the confusion, and the wreckage was hidden from sight. I found myself leaning over the back of my seat, clinging to the two terrified children. Jim let in the clutch and the car leapt forward, rounding a corner with a scream of tyres. As we accelerated again I heard firing break out behind us.

I turned to Jim and said, shakily, 'You didn't tell me you were using guns and bombs!'

'It wasn't my choice,' he replied tersely. 'The people in charge now seem to take it for granted—and we can't do without them.'

Only a few streets away he stopped the car abruptly outside what looked like an abandoned office block.

'Right, inside quickly!' he said.

We ran across the pavement and into the entrance hall. It was littered with sleeping bags, empty cans and bottles, odds and ends of personal possessions and the banisters had been torn away from the staircase, presumably to be used in a barricade. Four or five men were lounging among the debris. Jim spoke quickly to one of them who nodded and went out.

'He'll keep an eye on your car,' Jim said. 'Otherwise it probably wouldn't be there when we come out.'

He took us upstairs and into what was once, presumably, a secretary s office. Here another small group of men and girls were occupied with paper work of some kind. Once again Jim held a short, sotto voce conversation. A girl disappeared into the inner office. After a short wait we were summoned inside.

There were three men in the room. One tall, big built with a beer-drinker's stomach which overhung his trousers; the second younger with long, greasy dark hair which almost obscured his face as he sat with his head bent over a map. It was the third man, a slight, active-looking man with a narrow, clever face and very compelling blue eyes, who spoke, and as soon as he did so I understood Jim's reference to 'the Irishman'.

'What's this?' he asked sharply.

Jim explained. 'They tried to come through our check point. She says she's got to get through to Oxford, to visit someone. Apparently they didn't know about the situation round here.'

'Didn't know?' The Irishman looked me over with cool, impersonal eyes. "Where are you from?'

'Not very far away,' I said as casually as I could.

He came round his desk and moved closer to me.

'Look here. There's no point in us playing games with each other. If you were from anywhere round here you'd know what was going on. If you're trying to lie your way through it's one of two things. Either you're travelling without a permit—or you're a spy. Now which is it?'

Something bordering on a hysterical laugh caught at my throat. 'Do I look like a spy?'

'I've seen some unlikely looking spies in my time,' he returned, unmoved. 'If you're not, then what are you trying to do?'

I hesitated. Jim said,

'Look, you can talk to us. We're on the same side.'

I saw the Irishman shoot him a quick, contemptuous glance, but he said, 'Well, is he right?'

'How do I know?' I snapped. 'I don't want to be on anybody's side. I just want to get on with my own life.'

He leaned on the edge of his desk.

'Look, lady, if you wanted to do that you should have stayed at home. Right here there's only two sides. The fascist pigs who shoot down ordinary working men—and us. Now, if you want our help, you've got to be straight with us, and quickly. I've more important things to do and, God knows, not much time left to do them in.'

I took a long breath. 'All right, I'll tell you the whole story."

I told it, briefly, but leaving out nothing of significance. At the end Jim said,

'There you are, you see. We are on the same side.'

The Irishman was still looking at me. 'What about your husband?' he asked.

I looked away. 'He was killed, in the riot at Waterloo Station.'

The Irishman leaned forward and said sharply, 'What was his name?'

'Michael Fairing.'

I was aware that the information had caused a stir in the room. Everyone was looking at me. The Irishman straightened up and held out his hand to me.

'Mrs Fairing, your husband was one of the first martyrs in this struggle. If we can help, we'll do all we can.'

The thought flashed through my mind that it was odd that both Harrington and now this man should claim Mike as a martyr in their different causes, but I said nothing. From then on we were honoured guests. We were given chairs and brought cups of real coffee, something which we had not seen in our area for weeks. With the coffee came, luxury of luxuries, chocolate biscuits. It appeared that the occupation of the shopping precinct had yielded some stored up supplies, probably destined for the black market. While we ate and drank the Irishman pressed me for news of what was going on in my part of the country. There were, I gathered, various pirate radio stations on the air but their broadcasts were erratic and the information they gave confused and sometimes contradictory.

I said at one point, 'Surely you won't be able to hold out here much longer. What happens then?'

He shrugged. 'We move out and start again somewhere else. We're not getting much news through from the rest of the country but we did hear that resistance is holding up well around Birmingham and Coventry. We'll head for there when they flush us out of here.'

I put my hands through my hair. 'I had no idea that all this was going on. The country seems to be in chaos.'

'The government can't hold out much longer,' he said with an edge of triumph in his voice. 'Did you know that the Scots have declared independence? They've set up their own government in Edinburgh and most of the Scots regiments are supporting them.'

'My God!' I murmured. 'We're in the middle of a civil war!'

'It's the beginning of the Revolution!' he corrected me crisply. 'It's been a long time coming, but nothing can stop it now.'

We were silent for a while, then he said, 'Now, are you really determined to go on?'

I sighed. 'I don't see what else I can do. I'm terrified of the children being taken away if I go back.'

He nodded. 'Well, I can understand any woman wanting to keep her children out of the clutches of bastards like that. We'll do what we can to help you, but we can only get you out of the city. After that you're on your own. If you keep away from the towns you shouldn't come to any harm.' He turned to Jim. 'You go with them. Take them through our check points and get them as far north and west as you can. According to our last information there were army units here—and here . . .' They bent over the map. After a brief conference Jim straightened up.

'All right. I'll do my best. Are you ready?'

The Irishman shook hands with me.

'Good luck to you! I hope you get through.'

'Thanks,' I said. It was on the tip of my tongue to wish him luck too.

The car still stood outside, watched over by the student. The noise of the crowd had faded but we still heard occasional shots and distant explosions. Obviously the fighting had moved away. Jim drove fast through the deserted streets, stopping once at a barricade to identify himself. When we were beginning to leave the city behind he spoke for the first time.

'I'm sorry you had to go through all that. But if we'd let you go on someone else would have brought you in. We're trying to keep a fairly tight control over who goes in and out of the city.'

I said, 'Doesn't all this sicken you? The violence, I mean—bombs, guns, in an English city.'

'It wasn't my choice,' he muttered.

'But whose choice was it?' I asked. 'Who put those men in charge? That Irishman . . . he's not a student, or a worker.'

Jim gave me a brief, tight-lipped smile. 'No, you're right of course. He was the leader of an IRA cell based on Reading. When all this started, there he was, right on hand with all the necessary expertise and organization. He's

113

taken charge of the whole operation.'

I looked sideways at him. 'How do you feel—about working with the IRA?'

He pushed the car into a lower gear with sudden ferocity. 'They are not the only ones. IRA, Black September, Marxist revolutionaries, you name it, they're here. They are the only people who know how to cope with a situation like this—and the only people who can get us arms; and that's what we need if we're going to get rid of this government.'

'But surely they're only here to make the trouble worse,' I said. 'Does it have to be done their way?'

'Look,' he said. 'As I see it there are three possibilities. One—this government stays in power and we are reduced to the condition of Spain under Franco, or worse; because you needn't think that at the end of five years they are going to meekly let themselves be voted out again. Two—we wait for someone to "invite" the Warsaw pact countries, or the Cubans, to come and "liberate" us. Or three— we kick this government out ourselves; and to do that we need all the help we can get. Organizations like the IRA have international links. The Irishman says he can get us arms from Germany, or even from Japan. When we've got democracy back, then we'll see about dealing with the terrorists.'

He fell silent and I said no more. We came

to another check point. Jim got out and conferred briefly with the men there. Then he came back to the car.

'They say the army are only about two miles ahead. I'll do my best to get you through but no-one knows where the road blocks are.'

We drove on another mile or so. Then, as we approached a group of farm buildings the figure of a boy suddenly leapt out of the hedge and waved us urgently into an open gateway. Jim wrenched the wheel over and we rocked and bumped into the farm yard. We had just rounded the side of a barn, so that we were hidden from the roadway, when we heard the low roar of heavy engines approaching along the road. Through the branches of a hedge ahead of me I saw a column of tanks and armoured troop carriers grinding its way slowly past.

After a few words with the boy Jim drove on again. Shortly afterwards he pulled off the road by a pub and two men immediately came out. Once again Jim got out of the car and conferred with them. This time when he came back he did not get in but leaned down and spoke through the window.

'They say the road up ahead is clear, as far as they know. The army is obviously moving in towards the centre and it looks as if we've slipped through the ring. I'll have to leave you now and get back to the others. Will you be all right?'

I looked up at him. I had not realized until now what a comfort the presence of a man, even a stranger, had been. I swallowed.

'I expect so. We'll manage.'

He put his hand in through the window.

'Good luck. Take care.'

'And you,' I answered, taking his hand. 'Don't—don't get into danger unless you have to, will you. And thanks—for everything.'

He stood back and I shifted into the driving seat and started the engine. As the car slid out onto the road he waved and then turned away.

It occurred to me that I had no idea where we were, except that we had been heading roughly north-west. At the next junction there was a sign post. WANTAGE 4, it said. There had been no sound from the back of the car for some time. I stopped and looked round. Two solemn, pale faces stared back at me. I smiled at them.

'Cheer up! We're on our way now.'

They looked at me, unimpressed. Then Tim said plaintively,

'Could we have some lunch now?'

I looked at my watch. It was twenty minutes to one. Half the day gone, and we had covered only just over fifty of the two hundred and more miles to Dolgelly. Ahead an open gate let into a field. I pulled the car off the road and got out, my legs cramped and shaky from tension. The boys scrambled out after me. The wide, gently rolling Oxfordshire countryside was still and empty. The trees and hedges were still bare but there was a faint misting of green on the ploughland of the field and above us a skylark sang with rapturous urgency. Huge mounds of cumulus drifted overhead but we were in sunlight for the moment and there was very little wind. I smiled at the children.

'We'll have a picnic. Our first picnic of the year.'

Within half an hour we were back on the road. Perhaps it was the quietness of the countryside, or maybe just the effect of food and the release from tension, but I felt quite light-headed, almost a little drunk, though I had had no alcohol. Whatever it was I was no longer as alert as I should have been and we were on top of the road block before I realized it. There was an armoured car drawn half-way across the road and a jeep parked nearby, and a soldier was holding up his hand to halt us. I stopped, feeling sick with shock and disappointment. He came forward and looked in.

'Can I see your identity cards, please?' The tone was formal but not unpleasant.

Trying desperately to look unconcerned. I fumbled in my bag and produced the cards. He inspected them, glanced at my face and at the children, then said,

'Do you have a travel permit?'

'Travel permit?' I said stupidly.

He gazed at me dispassionately.

'You need a permit to travel more than twenty miles from the address on this card. By my reckoning you're about fifty miles from home. Can I see your permit, please?'

I swallowed. 'I haven't got one . . . I didn't realize . . .'

He opened my door. 'You'd better get out. Sergeant!'

As I got out another man appeared from behind the armoured car and came over to us. The soldier handed him our identity cards.

'Fifty miles from home and she hasn't got a travel permit, sarge,' he said laconically.

The sergeant inspected the cards and then turned to me. He had a cheerful, weathered face and his manner was kindly. Instinct told me that here was a man who might find a helpless woman very appealing.

'Where are you heading for, missus?' he asked.

I gave him a wide-eyed, desolate gaze.

'I'm trying to get to my parents' home in Wales. My mother's very ill. They need me.'

'Well, why didn't you get yourself a travel permit then?' he asked reasonably.

'I—I never thought. The message only came last night. I just packed and—set off.'

He shook his head and clicked his tongue.

'You've no business driving around this area with two kids. They'd have told you that if you'd applied for a permit—given you a safer route, most likely. I dunno. How you got this far without being stopped is a mystery to me.'

'I've got to get there,' I said, with a tone of urgent pleading which came easily. 'Please, couldn't you let me pass?'

He shook his head and pursed his lips. I had made a tactical error in asking him to break regulations.

'Can't do that, I'm afraid, missus. Against orders, you see. Now look, best thing you can do is go to the proper authorities and ask for a pass.'

'But where do I have to go?' I asked. 'It all takes time and I've got to hurry.'

'Well, you should have gone to your local police station,' he said, judiciously sucking in his cheeks. 'But I tell you what. Try the authorities in Oxford. There's a command post there. If you explain your reasons to them they might give you a permit to carry on. That's the best I can do for you, I'm afraid.'

I gazed into his face. I had never thought it was in me to wheedle and had despised what used to be called 'feminine wiles'.

'Couldn't you just forget you ever saw us? We'll be in Wales by tonight and no-one will ever know.'

Slowly he shook his head. 'Sorry, luv. Honest, it's for your own good. There are some very dodgy areas north of here, with some very funny people around. We couldn't guarantee your safety. I couldn't take the responsibility for letting you go off on your

119

own.' He turned and called 'Carter!'

Another private appeared. The sergeant addressed him.

'Get in the car and drive this lady and her children to the command post in Oxford, and then get back here on the double.'

Once again I moved over and let someone else drive. I could feel the children tense on the back seat but I was glad, at least, of their silence. After a bit I said innocently.

'What's going on then? Why are you blocking the roads?'

'Orders,' Carter said. Obviously he was not a great communicator. He was a thin young man with an outstanding crop of acne.

'But why?' I persisted. 'And why did your sergeant say it was dangerous to go on?'

'Commie rebels,' he replied, his tone flat and nasal. Then he added, 'They've been giving us a lot of trouble round here. The Russians have sent in a lot of agitators.'

'The Russians?' I queried.

'Oh ay,' he nodded without taking his eyes off the road. 'They want to start a civil war, see. So they can step in and take over.'

I was silent for a while. Then I said,

'I thought it was the trades unions, the workers—just wanting the right to strike and so on.'

He gave a low, catarrhal snort. 'You don't want to believe that. That's just white-wash. It's the reds that are behind it. Them, and the

Arabs.'

'But isn't it ordinary English workers that you're fighting?' I asked.

'Silly sod!' he said, then automatically, ' 'Scuse language. Don't know when they're well off. Lazy buggers! I'd give them strike! They ought to be in the army.'

I left it at that and lapsed into weary silence. We came to the outskirts of Oxford and it was apparent at once that the whole city was an armed camp. Along the by-pass tanks and troop carriers were parked almost nose to tail and almost the only vehicles moving were military ones. On open areas I saw field guns deployed, their crews lounging round them.

We passed through several road blocks and came into the centre of the city. I had always had a favourite fantasy about going to Oxford University and had spent happy days sight-seeing there. Now there were sentries outside the college gateways and armoured cars at every intersection. The usually thronged streets were empty, a tank was parked on Magdalen bridge and there was an army encampment in Christ Church meadows. As far as I could tell the ancient buildings were undamaged, but as in Reading the streets were littered with signs of conflict—broken windows, burnt out cars and torn up paving stones.

As we turned into the Broad the atmosphere abruptly changed. The streets were cleared of debris, banners and bunting were being put up, all red, white and blue with the initials of the NUP and the KBG prominent. A platform was being erected and crash barriers being put up.

'What's going on here?' I asked.

Carter shrugged. 'Search me.'

We drew up outside a police station which appeared to have been taken over, at least partially, by the Army. Armed sentries stood on guard by the main door and a sergeant was checking everyone who entered. Carter explained tersely,

'Lady needs a travel permit, sarge.' Then he nodded briefly in my direction and left.

The sergeant handed us on to a police constable, who said,

'Have a bit of a wait, I'm afraid. Take a seat over there, will you.'

We sat down with a number of other people on benches along one wall. A clerk at a desk was calling people up one by one and apparently taking down their particulars. These he handed to another man who disappeared with them through some swing doors, while the applicant returned to his seat. From time to time the man returned and beckoned someone from the queue. Judging from the intervals between such events we were in for a long wait. Tim leaned against me.

'Do we have to wait, Mummy?'

'I'm afraid so, darling.'

We sat on for almost an hour. Once I was called to the desk to show my identity card and explain my business, but that was all. The boys grew restless and fretful. I tried to talk to them to occupy their minds, but there was little conversation among the others waiting and we felt foolish and conspicuous when we spoke.

Suddenly there was a sound of sirens outside and the noise of engines. Simon jumped up and looked through a window.

'There are some cars coming—big cars—and some soldiers on motor-bikes. And a police car in front with its light flashing.'

I was aware of a sudden flurry of activity in the station and several officers, both police and army, came quickly through the swing doors. The sirens moaned into silence outside and someone opened the doors wide. Everyone's eyes turned to see who was coming in.

Simon cried out, 'Mummy, I can see Clare! It's Clare, Mummy!'

A moment later Jocelyn Wentworth came into the station, surrounded by officers and aides in civilian dress. Clare was close behind him, carrying a dispatch case. The party stopped in the middle of room to be greeted by the waiting officers.

I had come to my feet, my throat dry and closed. Should I try to attract Clare's attention? Or would that be the worst thing I could do?

While I stood paralyzed with indecision the party moved on towards the swing doors. Jocelyn's face was at its most austere and commanding, his eyes, more sunken than ever, passed over the antics of his hosts as they fell over each other in sycophantic courtesy. As they were about to pass through the doors Tim suddenly shouted,

'Aunty Clare! It's dust! Aunty Clare!'

Clare turned for an instant in the doorway. I knew she had seen us but her face gave no clue to her reaction. Then she followed the rest through the doors.

I said shakily, 'I don't know if you should have done that, Tim.'

'Why not?' he said. 'She didn't know we were here, did she.'

We sat down again, aware of curious glances from the others. I was trembling and my head ached. In the midst of my anxiety I found myself thinking 'I'd give anything for a cup of tea!' The children were nagging me with questions about what Clare was doing here and why she had not spoken to us. I wondered about the reason for her presence too. It seemed likely that Jocelyn was to be the chief guest at some kind of victory rally to celebrate the downfall of the Oxford militants. I thought bitterly of Clare's arrival in contrast to my own, borne along in the wake of Jocelyn's power and prestige, marked out now more than ever as a member of a dominant caste. It occurred to me that she probably had a good deal of power of her own, and to wonder how she would exercise it in our direction.

Some time later a soldier appeared and spoke to the man behind the desk. He looked up and called,

'Mrs Fairing?'

I went over, the children following.

'This way, please.'

The soldier led us through the swing doors and up a flight of stairs. We waited, the children clutching my hands, while he knocked at the door and looked in.

'Mrs Fairing is here.'

Then he stood back and signalled us to enter.

Clare was sitting behind a desk on which was the brief case and several piles of papers. She sat back as we came in and ran her hand over her smoothly brushed hair, looking at me with something close to exasperation.

'Nell, what on earth are you doing here?'

I studied her face. Under the careful make-up she looked tired, almost haggard. I looked at the hard lines of her mouth and knew that I could not afford to be completely honest.

'I'm trying to get to my parents' place in Wales,' I said. 'My mother has had a heart attack. I must go and look after her.'

Clare frowned at me and then looked down at a paper on her desk.

'Apparently you are travelling without a

permit.'

'Yes. I just didn't think about it. After all, we're not used . . .'

'Really, Nell, you infuriate me!' She rose abruptly and moved round the desk. 'Can't you realize even now that things have changed? I told you months ago that it would have to happen. We are in the middle of the greatest national emergency in our history and you expect to go trapesing around the country as if nothing had happened!'

She broke off and made another swift pass at her hair. As the interview went on I realized that this had become a habitual gesture, a reaction to any stress or indecision. Then she turned back to the desk, saying,

'Oh, sit down for heaven's sake! We'd better have some tea.'

She pressed a button on the intercom and ordered tea and, as an afterthought, orange for the boys. I sank down into a chair, feeling that some semblance of normality had been restored.

Clare resumed her seat also and said,

'Now, what's all this about your mother?'

'She's had a heart attack. I've got to go and nurse her.'

'When did you hear this?'

'Last night. My father telephoned.'

'Telephoned?' Clare's beautifully defined eyebrows rose fractionally. 'I'm surprised he got through. The telephone service is

126

supposed to be for emergencies only for the time being.'

'I know,' I replied hastily. 'I suppose he must have persuaded someone that this was an emergency.' In fact I had made several attempts to contact my parents by phone in the last weeks without success. Letters also failed to arrive. I had put this down to general disruption but I saw now that it was all part of the government's policy of preventing people from finding out what was going on in the rest of the country.

'But surely your mother is in hospital if the attack was serious,' Clare was saying.

'Oh she is,' I agreed, wondering desperately where the nearest hospital was. 'But not for long. It wasn't that serious. They are letting her go home in a day or two. That's why I must be there.'

'They won't let her out until she's able to manage,' Clare said firmly. 'Hospital staff aren't fools, you know. They know how difficult it is for people to travel at the moment. They will keep her in if you're not there to look after her.'

'But there's my father, too,' I protested.

'Surely he can take care of himself.'

'But it's very lonely up there. I don't like to think of him all by himself. Suppose he had a fall or something . . .'

Once again Clare's hand went to her hair.

'Stop imagining the worst, Nell. It's typical

of you, working yourself up into a state without having really thought things through. There are all sorts of agencies whose job it is to keep an eye on old people. The hospital will see to it that your father and your mother get all the help they need. It's the government's declared policy to see that all the social services are maintained, for those that really need them. The best thing you can do is to go back home with the boys and wait until you hear from your father again.'

The tea arrived at that moment; strong, bitter canteen tea, but welcome just the same. As soon as the policeman who brought it had withdrawn I said,

'But Clare, what's the point in me going back now? I'm well on my way, and turning back would just be a waste of petrol. Couldn't you arrange a permit for us?'

'I'm afraid it's out of the question,' she said sharply, shifting papers on her desk.

'Why?' I demanded.

She looked at me. 'Why? I can think of a dozen reasons, and so could you if you used your brains instead of your emotions for once. Do I have to keep telling you that we have a State of Emergency? What is needed at this point in time is for every single person to get on quietly and conscientiously with his or her job. You should be at home, seeing that your children go to school. What's going to happen to their schooling up in Wales? Have you thought about that? Then there must be dozens of things you could usefully do in your area. I don't suppose it's occurred to you to contact your local KBG headquarters and see if you can help in any way.'

'As a matter of fact I have,' I said. The opportunity to score off Clare was irresistible. Then I could have bitten off my tongue. Suppose Clare decided to contact Harrington and check up on me . . .

She stared at me for a moment and then went on, less brusquely,

'Well, I'm glad to hear it. I hadn't expected you to show that much initiative. Well then, you know how valuable your help could be. You should be concentrating on that.'

'I really am worried about my mother, Clare. Suppose she had another attack. I want to see her again . . . in case anything happens.'

In silence she picked up her tea cup and put it down again, untasted. Then she said casually,

'How's Alan?'

I realized with a shock that she must assume that Alan was still staying with us.

'I don't know, Clare,' I replied quietly. 'He left-the day Mike was killed. He—never knew about Mike.'

She stared at me. 'Left? Where for?'

'I don't know. He didn't tell me he was going, but he left a note saying he'd gone to look for work. He didn't say where.' I thought

129

of telling her about the suits left in the wardrobe but something stopped me.

Clare sat twiddling a pen in one hand, the other stroking her sleek, dark head, gazing down at her desk. I wondered what she was feeling. At length she pulled herself together and straightened up.

'Look, I'll get you a permit made out that will get you back home. Believe me, it's the best thing for all of you.'

She reached for the intercom. I jumped up and moved quickly to the desk.

'Clare, I don't want to go home!' I spoke angrily, almost through clenched teeth and she stopped and looked at me in surprise. For a moment we held each other's eyes. Then she said sharply,

'All right! I shouldn't tell you this but I know how bloody obstinate you can be, so sit down and listen. Maybe I can get you to understand something about the situation we're in, and then, perhaps, you'll co-operate.'

I sat down again, a little disturbed at the outburst, and she rose and began to prowl about the room. I was aware more clearly than ever of the strain and tension which had reached something close to breaking point.

'I suppose you've been living in your usual cosy little cloud-cuckoo-land, putting your head in the sand and trying to pretend that everything is really normal—or soon will be!' I thought of Mike's death and the constant

130

sense of Harrington and his friends watching me; of the builder's yard and the burnt surgery and Jane's children being dragged away; and I bit back an angry protest at the injustice of the remark. I doubt if Clare would have heard it anyway. She was well into her stride now. 'You've been fortunate in that you happen to be living in a part of the country where things are more or less normal. If you knew what Jocelyn has been trying to cope with! The General Strike was only the beginning, of course, We expected that. Jocelyn has always said that one day we would have to have a show-down with the unions, and that when it came the rest of the country would back us, But none of us realized how strong the subversive forces in the country had become! It was like the dragon's teeth! They sprang up all over the country—the agitators who thought they saw the opportunity they had been waiting for to start a revolution; and the others, the unholy alliance, all the terrorist gangs who thought they stood to gain something from the end of democracy.' The words were spilling out now, bitten off in rapid, staccato phrases. She was re-living a trauma, not talking to me. 'Of course, we know that a lot of them were infiltrators from Warsaw Pact countries. That's where the arms have come from too. And it's become clear why the Left were continually agitating to have our defence expenditure reduced. With the army reduced to a skeleton we simply haven't got the resources to hold the violence in check all over the country. And the people are such fools! Oh there are some areas, of course, where we can rely on them to co-operate with the local KBG; but in the cities they've allowed themselves to be led by the nose by the very people who have been trying to ruin this country for years. Places like Liverpool and Birmingham have become ungovernable. The workers have seized the factories and barricaded the city centres. Every University in the country has been occupied by the students, and a lot of schools, too. The Scots have declared themselves independent, of course. Well, they can stew in their own juice for a while and see how they get on without subsidies from Westminster! The Welsh Nationalists have started a guerrilla campaign, concentrating on sabotaging water supplies for the Midlands, and now that the army has been withdrawn the Irish Unionists are solving the problem of the Catholic minority in the way they have been wanting to for years. We've had to concentrate on holding London and the south-east. We're in complete control south of Coventry and everywhere east of the Severn. At the moment we're establishing a line from Worcester through Northampton and up to the Wash to prevent infiltrators moving in from further north. The only places in this area where we were still having real trouble were Oxford and Reading. Well we've got Oxford under control, as you can see. In a day or two Reading will be quiet too. But you see why I can't let you go on any further.'

She returned abruptly to her chair and looked at me, quite composed again, as if all that she had said was a statement of simple fact. I stared back at her, feeling myself physically sagging in my chair.

'Do you mean to say that the whole country is in anarchy, apart from this area?'

She shrugged slightly. 'It varies, of course. Many rural areas are perfectly quiet and life is going on more or less normally. There are others, in some of the more remote districts, which have declared themselves autonomous and tried to set up their own local government—refusing to pay taxes or obey the emergency regulations. They'll come to heel sooner or later when they discover they just can't exist as separate units. Food supplies are getting very short. With so many of the ports out of action and internal transport disrupted it's becoming impossible to keep supplies going. Things are going to be very hard soon, especially in the cities.'

'So what is going to happen?' I asked. 'I mean, what do you plan for the future.'

She straightened herself in the chair, as if I had triggered some conditioned reflex. 'We shall consolidate our hold on this area and then move north. By that time the violence should have burnt itself out to a large extent. People will begin to want order and peace, above all food. They will be prepared to defy the extremists and support the elected government.'

We met each other's eyes, then she looked away and said wearily, 'Go home, Nell. You'll be much better off there.'

She pressed the intercom button and told someone to make out a travel permit for me and the boys and bring it in. In the defeated silence which followed the two boys scuffled over the last biscuit. I said,

'Why is Jocelyn here?'

'He's making a speech tonight. There is going to be a big rally in support of the Government—to show that Oxford is really loyal, in spite of the troubles.'

I looked at her. For the first time there was a faint hint of irony in her eyes.

'Suppose nobody comes to it?' I asked.

She smiled faintly. 'They'll come!'

A police woman came in with a piece of paper. Clare took it, filled in one or two details and signed it. Then she held it out to me. It was quite explicit. We were to be allowed to travel by a clearly defined route back to where we had started.

Clare said, 'You realize I shouldn't really do this. I should hand you over to the police to be charged with breaking the emergency regulations. The penalties are quite severe,

134

you know.' She paused. I kept my eyes on the paper. If she was expecting thanks, she was out of luck. She went on, in the authoritative, 'it's-all-for-your-own-good' tone which had always infuriated me, 'Go on, Nell. It's the best thing. If you start now you'll be home by the boys' bedtime.' Then, to the police-woman, 'Show Mrs Fairing down to her car, will you.'

'Clare . . .'

She looked up at me bleakly. 'Well?'

I hesitated.

'Any message for Alan if he turns up?'

With careful deliberation she moved her untouched tea-cup back onto the tray.

'No, I don't think so. There isn't anything I could say that would be—relevant, anymore.'

Ten minutes later we were driving out of the city on the road towards Abingdon. We passed through several check points and the careful scrutiny given to my pass soon killed any ideas I had of trying to use it in the wrong direction. I drove slowly, trying to think. It was possible, of course, that if we went home no one would know where we had been. Harrington might never discover my part in passing on information to Jane. If I settled down and pretended to be a diligent KBG worker perhaps we could ride out the storm until . . . Until what? Until the NUP were firmly in control of the whole country? Or until bloody revolution swept into our quiet suburbs too? Were we to live, like so many others I had read

135

of, in fear of a sudden knock on the door?

'South of Birmingham and East of the Severn' Clare had said. I stopped the car and got out the map. Forty odd miles away the government's writ ceased to run! If we could only cover those forty miles . . . I was tempted to turn the car round and make another attempt through the lanes, but I had seen how many check points there were in that area. The car was too conspicuous, too easily identified. If we were to disappear, so that our trail could not be picked up even if Clare decided to check on us, we must leave it. At that moment a bus appeared around a bend ahead of us. It seemed so incongruous after all that had happened, and yet so opportune, that I wondered for a second if I was suffering from some form of hallucination. As it approached I saw that the destination panel at the front bore the name Witney. Witney—I searched the map. That was north of where I was now, about what—fifteen miles distant. What happened to buses at a check point? Did they go through the identity of each passenger? The bus was quite full—people going home from work, I supposed. It would take a long time to check them all at each road block.

I started the engine and wrenched the steering wheel hard round. It took only a few seconds to catch up with the bus. I followed it back to the last road block and parked a hundred yards away. It was too far to see exactly what happened, but the bus was stationary for less than two minutes and I had seen only one soldier enter it.

Once again I turned the car and retraced my route until a bus stop came into view. Ignoring the fretful questions from the back seat I got out and crossed the road to look at the time-table. If, in this improbable normality, the buses were running to schedule there should be another in half an hour. I went back to the car and drove it some way up a side road and then into a little copse.

When I explained my plans to the boys their tired faces fell.

'I thought we were going home!' Tim said miserably, while Simon added sceptically,

'We can't get all the way to Granny's on a bus.'

'How do you know?' I cried, with a kind of crazy optimism. 'We can try, can't we?'

I opened the boot and began pulling out cases and boxes. The thought of abandoning half our possessions in the middle of a wood like this seemed the ultimate lunacy, but I closed my mind to it and concentrated on reducing my load to one suitcase and a shopping bag full of food. I gave the boys the last of the bread and a piece of cheese each, reasoning that we might as well eat what we could not carry.

When I had finished I loaded everything else into the boot and locked it, though with what object I was not sure. Then, as an afterthought, I got out the tool kit and, with a struggle, succeeded in removing the number plates. A short excursion into the wood revealed a stream, thickly overhung with brambles. I dropped the plates into it and pulled the brambles across the place where they lay. Then I called the boys to me and we headed for the bus stop.

When the bus drove into sight, only two or three minutes late, it made me feel as if what I had just done was part of a ridiculous charade. I signalled it and it drew up beside us, purring and panting like a large, friendly animal. I gave the driver some money.

'One and two halves to Witney, please.'

The boys cantered happily to the vacant rear seat and flopped down. Buses were a comparative novelty to them.

At the first road block I clutched my bags and felt dizzy with the beating of my own heart. A soldier boarded the bus and spoke to the driver. Then he gave a cursory glance down the length of the vehicle and, almost unbelievably got off again and waved us on,

As I relaxed I caught Simon's eye. Silently I found his hand and pressed it.

The bus growled along, warm and tobacco smelling, full of women with shopping baskets and men in working clothes. I began to relax. We were on our way again.

Dusk was beginning to fall as we drew into a

little town of broad streets and stone houses. I realized that if we were going to find accommodation for the night before the curfew started we should have to hurry. At the bus stop a policeman stood by the door as the people descended. I saw that they were showing their identity cards but the constable was only taking a cursory glance at each one. I gave Simon the shopping bag to carry and took out our cards, holding them in my free hand so that the address was hidden. Then, with the two boys behind me, I joined the line of passengers. We stepped down and I held the cards up towards the policeman. He glanced at them, looked behind me at the children, and turned his attention to the next passenger on the line. We walked briskly away down the main street.

A hundred yards or so further on I stopped and put down the case. The boys stood and looked at me expectantly. Tim whined,

'I'm tired! Can we go to a restaurant and have a meal?'

'Where are we going to stay tonight?' Simon asked. 'It's getting dark.'

The brief rush of optimism which I had felt on the bus evaporated. The day seemed to have gone on for ever. My head ached and I was exhausted.

'I don't know, Simon,' I said, looking round. 'I'll have to think. Just be quiet a minute, like good boys.'

139

Along the street I could see two hotels. Suppose I just walked in and booked a room? They would want identity cards. Would they also want travel permits? Anyway, suppose Clare had been checking up on us, or suppose the car had been found. Hotels would be the first place for inquiries to be made if anyone was looking for us. It was not worth the risk, I decided. But if not a hotel, then where? A private house, somewhere that offered bed and breakfast, perhaps? But how did we find one? I had seen no helpful signs as we came into the town. One thing was certain, we were only making ourselves conspicuous standing here.

'Come on. We'll walk on a bit,' I said, picking up the case.

'I don't want to walk. I'm tired!' wailed Tim.

I restrained the sharp answer that rose to my lips and said,

'I know, darling. We all are. Just a bit further.'

We came to a side street and my nose spelled out an unmistakable message. Further down the street lighted windows misted with steam confirmed it.

'Fish and chips!' I said, 'Come on, we'll get some.'

The shop was empty except for a middle-aged couple silently consuming their fish and chips with their eyes on the television set in one corner. I told the boys to sit down at a table and they, too, became immediately hypnotised. I went to the counter and gave my order.

'Eat here or take away?' the man serving asked, reluctantly putting aside a newspaper which seemed to have more pictures of scantily clad girls than print. One way of getting round the censorship laws, I supposed.

'Eat here, please,' I replied. At least we could sit here for a while and I could think.

'Ration books?' he said.

'What?'

'Ration books.' He put out his hand and opened and closed the fingers meaningfully.

'Oh, how silly of me!' I exclaimed. 'We don't usually eat out. I hadn't thought.'

I produced the ration books. He leafed through them with greasy fingers, tore out some coupons and then looked at the address on the front.

'Long way from home,' he said, non-committally.

'Yes,' I smiled brightly. 'On our way to visit my parents.'

He grunted and turned away to put three pieces of fish on plates. Then he put the plates down, gave the pan of chips a cursory shake and put it back into the hot fat and then disappeared into the back of the shop. I thought I heard the faint ding of a telephone being picked up. I looked round, wondering whether I should gather up the children and disappear into the night. No, that would look very suspicious. Better to wait. But who was he ringing? When he came back I said,

'Look, I'm sorry. I think we'd better take it with us after all. I hadn't realized how late it is.'

He looked at me and raised his eyebrows.

'Oh ah?' Then he turned away, muttering something about 'want to make up your mind' and shovelled fish and chips into bags. I paid him and went quickly to the children. They protested miserably at being dragged away from the television and out into the streets again. Tim began to cry, saying,

'I hate this. I wish we'd never come. We ought to have stayed at home.'

Eventually we found a bench in a little public garden and sat huddled together, eating the food with our fingers. While the boys were quiet I struggled with the problem of where we should spend the night. Travelling like this it could take days to reach Dolgelly but I shrank from the risk of going to a hotel, or even of presenting our ration books again. It occurred to me sickeningly that I had made myself into a homeless vagrant whose children might well be taken into care, and with some justification. Added to this it would soon be completely dark and we were violating the curfew.

Desperately I looked around me. A short distance away stood a church. Recollections of the law of sanctuary flickered through my head. Could we spend the night in there? Cold comfort for my weary children! But if there was a church, there must be a vicar or a rector, or a minister of some sort, living nearby. Was it too trite and romantic an idea to believe that a man of religion could not refuse us hospitality? I made a decision born out of sheer desperation.

'Come on, kids. We're going to find somewhere to stay now.'

They dragged themselves to their feet and followed me. I walked as far as the church. Outside was a board giving times of services and, underneath, the name of the minister, the Rev. Philip Woodstock. We found the house next to the church. I marched straight up to it and rang the doorbell.

It was answered by an attractive, untidy woman perhaps a little older than myself. As soon as the door opened I said,

'I'm very sorry to bother you, but I need help. Could I possibly speak to the vicar?'

She took us in with a quick glance and stood back with a lack of hesitation which surprised me, saying 'Come in, please,' and at once closed the door quietly behind us. Then she crossed the hall and opened another door into a lighted room.

'This way, please.' She smiled at me, then turning into the room added, 'Someone needs help, Philip.'

I went in, feeling Tim's hand slipped into

143

mine. The room was furnished with old, well-worn furniture and fabrics with William Morris prints; a room of warm colours and gleaming polished wood, which reflected the glow of a log fire. The Rev. Woodstock, his dog-collar protruding above the neck of an equally well-worn sweater, was just rising from an armchair.

'Come in, come in. Come and sit down. I'm Philip Woodstock, and this is my wife, Jenny.'

There was no surprise in his voice. I shook hands with him, feeling suddenly as if I had stepped outside my body and was watching myself from a distance.

'My name is Eleanor Fairing. These are my children, Simon and Tim. I'm sorry to intrude on you like this.'

'Not at all,' he exclaimed. 'Do sit down. Jenny, could we have some tea, do you think? And some warm milk for the boys? Have you had anything to eat?'

'Yes, thank you,' I answered, and Tim, who was as instinctive as a dog in his reactions to people, said,

'We've just had some fish and chips.'

'Well, that's splendid, isn't it,' Philip Woodstock grinned. 'You come and have a warm by the fire then.'

He was in his middle thirties, I guessed, dark haired and round faced, with clear blue eyes behind large, dark-rimmed glasses. We seated ourselves and he dropped back into his chair and leaned towards me, clasping his hands between his knees.

'Now, where have you come from?' he inquired.

I blinked at him. 'You seem to know *why* we have come to you . . .'

He looked puzzled. 'I'm sorry, I'd assumed . . . You were directed here, weren't you?'

'No.' I shook my head. 'I came—well, out of desperation, I suppose.'

'Let's call it inspiration,' he said cheerfully. 'But you are looking for shelter for the night. Am I right?'

'Yes, you are,' I said. 'But I don't know how you guessed.'

'Never mind that for the moment. Just tell me your story.'

So I told it, without reservation, feeling that anything less than total frankness would break the spell and have us cast out again into the darkness. By the time I had finished Jenny Woodstock had returned and the boys were growing heavy-eyed over their hot milk.

'Right. First things first,' said the vicar. 'You are very welcome to spend the night here and you will be perfectly safe, so please don't have any worries on that score. Now, it looks as if these two young men are about ready for bed, so shall we get them settled first?'

Jenny took us upstairs and helped me to settle the boys in a big double bed, then left me to say goodnight to them. I gave them both a long hug.

'I'm sorry it's been such a nasty day, loves. Let's hope tomorrow will be better.'

Simon looked up at me, snug among white sheets.

'You can't help it, Mum,' he said. 'I expect you wish Daddy was here to look after us, don't you?'

I hugged him again to hide my face and then escaped quickly into my own room.

After a while I washed and tidied myself and went down again to the sitting room. The relief of having found shelter was like the gentle onset of some pain-killing drug and I felt lethargic and slightly shaky. The vicar and his wife fussed over me, seating me by the fire and pressing me to accept more food or another hot drink. I knew well enough the strain on the rations of feeding extra mouths and refused but when Philip Woodstock produced a bottle of brandy and insisted I must have some 'for medicinal purposes' I weakened. After I had taken a sip or two he said,

'So you really happened to knock at our door quite by chance?'

'Yes,' I replied. 'I was afraid to try a hotel. I just took a gamble that a minister wouldn't turn me over to the authorities. But I take it I'm not the first.'

The husband and wife glanced at each other briefly, their faces sombre.

'Far from it,' Philip said. 'I take it you know what has been going on in this area.'

'You mean the riots and street fighting in Oxford and Reading? I only found out when I tried to drive through today. We had no idea where I live how bad it was elsewhere.'

He nodded. 'No-one knows much about the rest of the country, but we have become a kind of staging post for people getting out of Oxford. It's been quiet here. Everyone has obeyed the regulations and more or less accepted the situation. Besides which the local KBG are pretty active and well supported. Anyone trying to raise a protest has been dealt with in a fairly summary fashion.'

'I've had some experience of that in my area,' I put in.

He went on. 'We heard about the riots in Oxford, and then we saw the troops moving in. It was after that we had our first—refugee is the only word for it, I suppose. I found him in the church one evening. He was a lecturer from the University—quite a prominent man. I won't tell you his name, but it is one that you would probably recognize. He had been instrumental in organizing the resistance and when it was clear that they couldn't hold out much longer his students persuaded him to get out. He would have been a marked man once the authorities took over and they felt he could be more useful free than in prison. We gave him a bed for the night and sent him on his way. He must have somehow got word back into the city, because a night or two later we had another lecturer on our doorstep, with his whole family—wife and two very small children.'

'Where did they go, after leaving here?' I asked.

'West,' he answered, 'the way fugitives have always headed in Britain—west and north, into the mountains. Our communications are not much better than in your part of the country but we do hear rumours from time to time. Also there's a pirate radio station I can sometimes pick up, when it's not being jammed. Apparently the industrial midlands are in a state of virtual rebellion, mostly in the hands of workers' revolutionary councils and such like, with pockets where the KBG are holding out. The Cotswolds are crawling with army units and Cheltenham is a KBG stronghold with Civil Militia patrols on every street comer. But, according to what we hear, and I must stress it is only rumour, on the other side of the Severn, round the forest of Dean, they have made what amounts to a UDI. They are refusing to accept any orders from the present government and have raised a force to hold all the river crossings from the Severn Tunnel up to Gloucester. Of course, they couldn't hold out for long if the government sent in troops but I get the impression that the army has got too much on

148

its plate just now to worry over much about such a relatively unimportant area. Anyway, that's where the others were headed for, hoping to find a temporary sanctuary, if nothing more. But I must emphasize again that these are only rumours.'

'I can confirm some of them,' I told him, and related my interview with Clare. He listened intently, nodding from time to time.

'So things really are that bad,' he said when I had finished. He leant back in his chair and stared into the fire and I saw on his face the same weary disbelief that I had seen on so many others that day. He shook his head. 'The economists and the political observers have been warning us for years that this could happen, but even up to a couple of months ago I never believed it would. Hardship, yes—but not this choice between a totalitarian government and anarchy.'

'None of us did,' I replied quietly.

He returned his attention to me. 'Anyway, the best suggestion I can give you is to head in the same direction. If you can get across the Severn you should find people who will help you on your way. Now. I know a young chap who drives a lorry for a local market gardener. He goes to Gloucester pretty well every day and he's willing to help people like you. If we put you in the back, behind some crates and under a tarpaulin, can you be sure that your boys won't give themselves away if you're stopped?'

I remembered the petrified silence in the back of the car on one or two occasions that day and said,

'Yes, I can be pretty confident about that.'

'Very well, then,' he continued. 'I'll get in touch with this lad and see if he can take you on tomorrow.'

He fetched an ordnance survey map and spread it out on the table.

'He'll drop you—here, where the Cheltenham–Stroud road crosses the A436 into Gloucester. After that I'm afraid you'll have to go on on foot. I should head for here if I were you. His finger indicated a broad loop of the river. 'There's a ferry marked across to Newnham. Obviously it won't still be running normally, but you might be able to persuade someone to take you across, or get a message over to the other side.'

He straightened up and looked at me. 'It's not a very encouraging prospect, I'm afraid, but it's the best I can do.'

I looked again at the map. By the tortuous side-roads which I would have to follow it must be all of sixteen or twenty miles to the ferry from the main road. Could the children walk that far? One did hear of them doing remarkable distances on sponsored walks—but under these circumstances? Well, we should just have to see.

Philip said, 'I can't give you the map, but I'll

make a tracing of that part for you. Then at least you'll be able to find your way.'

I shook my head. 'There's no need, thanks. I brought some maps with me. I've got this one in my case.'

'Well,' he gave me a small, approving smile, 'you obviously came prepared for a round about journey.'

I sighed. 'I hadn't reckoned on doing most of it on foot. I really believed that by now we'd be safely in my parents' house, you know.'

He touched my arm consolingly. 'Come and sit down again.'

When we were seated I said, 'Have you had any other people through here—since the professor and his family?'

His face darkened. 'We had a young chap a few days ago. He was quite a harmless, mild-mannered lad—not the firebrand type at all. He'd been picked up by the police during a street battle and accused of being one of the ring-leaders. They wanted the names of the people who were organizing the resistance and where they could be found. After twenty-four hours they handed him over to an army interrogation unit. I won't go into details about what they did to him. He told me that the unit had recently been recalled from Northern Ireland. He heard one of the officers say "Thank God we can get on with the job without some doddering government minister pussy-footing around because he's afraid the press will get hold of it." When they were convinced he really didn't know anything they drove him a few miles out of the city and pushed him out of the car. We had to keep him here three days before he was fit to go on.' He paused for a moment and then added, 'I think it was the most shattering experience of my life—realizing that such things can happen here. That the torturers are not a different breed of men . . .'

We were silent for a while. At length I said, 'It must be difficult for you. Aren't you afraid of what might happen, if you were found out?'

He got up and pushed a log back onto the fire with his foot and stood looking down at it, his hands thrust deep into his trouser pockets.

'Yes,' he said, without looking at me. 'I am, sometimes, very afraid. Specially since that last incident. And very disturbed, too. It goes against all my instincts to oppose the rule of law, but how can I refuse to help people like yourself, like that boy? Sometimes I feel I should be standing up in my pulpit denouncing the Government and urging my flock to resistance. How can I be sure that it is prudence and not cowardice that stops me? And yet, what useful purpose would it serve?' He looked at me and gave a small, self-deprecating smile. 'You see, I can't offer you great certainties or—or religious guidance. I'm as confused as you are.'

By morning the sense of unreality, of

existing in the dimension of dreams or of watching myself on film, which had repeatedly overtaken me on the previous day, had gone. As soon as we had eaten breakfast Philip led us through into the garage and opened the rear door of his elderly car.

'I hate to appear melodramatic,' he said apologetically, 'But would you mind crouching on the floor with a rug over you? There aren't any road blocks to pass but we do have the usual quota of nosey neighbours and I'm afraid the KBG like to encourage them.'

After a short drive the car stopped and Philip let us out into a yard surrounded by barns and outbuildings. The car was drawn up a few feet from the lowered tailboard of a lorry. A young man beckoned us quickly into its interior. The lorry was stacked with crates of vegetables and a space had been left in one place just large enough for us to sit in. We settled ourselves and Philip stacked our luggage at our feet. There were hasty goodbyes and an inadequate attempt at thanks and then the tailboard was fastened. A moment or two later we were on the move again.

It was not a pleasant journey. Our positions were cramped and the hard floor of the lorry jarred our bones, while the smell of cabbage grew quite sickening in the confined space. However, for me the sense of forward movement compensated for all the discomforts. Every two minutes was another mile of our journey behind us and I would quite happily have stayed where I was all day, if that would have got us to Wales and my parents' house.

We were stopped once and I heard the driver being questioned about his load and his destination but it was obvious that he was known and the questions took the form of friendly chaff. It never occurred to anyone to check the load. I thanked God, as we pulled away, that we were, as a nation, inexperienced in such matters.

Soon afterwards we stopped again and after a moment the driver's voice spoke casually from outside the lorry.

'I'll have to drop you here. We've just crossed the Cheltenham road. That's where the check point was. If you walk on from here and take the next on the left you can get back onto the main road to Stroud at Castle Hill.' A match rasped as he lit a cigarette. 'There's no-one about. I'll come round and undo the tailboard. Then I want you to nip out as quick as you can. O.K.?'

'O.K.'

I squirmed round and gathered up our things and we squeezed between the crates to the rear of the lorry. A moment later we were outside on the verge in the bright March sunlight. The driver slammed the tailboard shut and said, without looking at us,

'Cheer-oh, then. Good luck!'

A moment later the lorry had disappeared round a bend.

We began to walk. Tim said,

'Is it going to be very far?'

'Yes,' I said firmly. 'Further than you've ever walked in your life.'

He sighed. 'You know I hate long walks!'

I said, with a touch of asperity, remembering all too well his moans and protests when he grew tired of walking, 'Well, it won't be any good saying "I can't walk any further" or "I want to go home" because it will be a question of going on or spending the night in a field, probably. So you'd better make up your mind that you can walk—a lot further than you think.'

All day we plodded through the lanes which skirted the edge of the Cotswolds, heading always west towards the Severn. The weather began clear and sunny but by mid-afternoon it had clouded over and a steady drizzle began to fall. The suitcase which I carried was heavy and made me feel conspicuous. At a little village store I purchased two pounds of carrots and a paper carrier to put them in. In a field farther on I emptied out the carrots and crammed our most essential belongings into the carrier. Everything else went into a ditch to be covered with brambles and dead leaves.

By late afternoon we had crossed the M5 and were in the flat, wind-swept pasture land

155

of the estuary. There was a continuous coming and going of helicopters overhead and it was clear that they were patrolling the river. Once one dropped low over us and appeared to be inspecting us. Once again I was oppressed by the sheer lunacy of what we were doing, fleeing like stateless refugees in our own country. Tim was whimpering and complaining that his feet hurt and Simon was dragging an infuriating ten yards behind. I stopped under the shelter of a single oak tree and gave them the last of the food. It was little enough. We had eaten most of it at lunch time.

I took off Tim's shoes and looked at his feet. His heel was badly blistered, the flesh showing raw through the broken skin. I could only hug him and apologise for not attending to his complaints before, and then bandage the foot awkwardly with my handkerchief and ease it back into his shoes.

I looked at my watch. It was almost five. Another hour and a half until curfew, and the ferry was perhaps four miles away. If we kept going, what were the chances of finding a boat? And even if we did, dare I attempt the river crossing at night? Vague notions about tides and currents filled my mind. Admittedly, there would be less chance of being spotted by the helicopter patrols, but equally we might be picked up for breaking the curfew before we even reached the river. Anyway, could the children walk another four miles?

Simon said, 'Where are we going to sleep tonight?'

Squatting on the damp ground with my arm still round Tim I looked up at him.

'I don't know, Simon. I don't think we dare go to anyone's house tonight. It would be awful to get sent back after we've walked all this way, wouldn't it? I think when it's nearly dark we'll have to look for a barn or something where we can spend the night. If we can find some nice, dry hay we'll soon be warm and comfortable.'

He continued to stare down at me.

'That means that there won't be any supper. Or any breakfast tomorrow.'

Tim began to cry again. 'I'm hungry! I want some supper. I wish we'd never come here. I wish we'd stayed at home!'

I glared at Simon.

'Why can't you keep your stupid mouth shut?'

For a moment longer he held my gaze. Then he bent down and took Tim by the arm.

'Come on, Tim. Don't cry. It'll be all right—I expect.'

He drew him to his feet and pulled his arm over his own shoulder. They stood together looking down at me, Tim's face streaked with tears. Then they turned and began to trudge on along the road. I gathered up the bags and followed them, my throat aching with my own unshed tears.

As we went on my mind obsessively explored the problem of food. I could go without, I knew, although my stomach was hollow. So could the children, I supposed, if necessary, though my instincts rebelled at the idea. Whatever happened we must drink. The idea of hot soup returned again and again, impairing my ability to work at the question logically, getting between me and reality. Ahead the road crossed a little bridge. Screwing my eyes up against the rain and the gathering dusk I saw that it spanned a small river. Well, we could drink there. Years of conditioning rose in revolt and murmured "pollution" in my brain. I called the children to me and we scrambled through a fence and down to the bank. The river ran sluggishly in a muddy bed edged with reeds. I stooped and managed to scoop up a handful of water, It tasted of wet earth. I scooped some up for Tim, who drank it and made a face. Simon got some water to his mouth and then spat it out again. After a few mouthfuls we had all had enough. As we scrambled back to the road I reflected bitterly on our incapacity for existing, even at the most basic level, without the aids of civilization.

Ahead, I knew from my map, was another small village. We must find some form of shelter there. I looked again at my watch. Just after six. Tim was sniffing rhythmically as he walked, his weeping now reduced to a kind of automatic reflex. I could hear Simon's teeth chattering.

'Just a bit further,' I encouraged them.

Headlights appeared in front of us. I drew the boys hastily into the side of the road. The oncoming vehicle drew closer, slowed and came to a standstill just before reaching us so that we were fixed, like rabbits, in the glare of its lights. I could just make out the outlines of a Land Rover. A man swung down from the passenger seat and as he came forward into the light I saw the Civil Militia arm-band and the rifle slung on his shoulder.

'Identity cards, please.'

The harsh curtness of the voice did not succeed in masking either the local burr or the youth of its owner. Outlined against the headlights I guessed him to be a local farm worker. Still, whatever his age or his regular occupation, the band on his arm and the rifle on his shoulder made him the voice of authority. As if someone had pulled out some psychological plug I felt the last reserves draining out of me. For an instant I contemplated seizing the boys and running. Instead I heard myself saying,

'Identity cards? What do you want them for?'

'Because I don't know you, missus,' he replied tersely. 'And because I'd like to know what you're doing around these parts at this time of night.'

Somewhere up the road a dog began barking and then was suddenly silent. I groped in my bag, pretending to hunt for the cards, desperately trying to think of some way out of showing them.

'Come on!'

The man had unslung his rifle from his shoulder. I said, suddenly furious,

'Put that thing away! You don't really think you're going to shoot us, do you? A woman and two children, walking harmlessly along a country road? This is England—remember?'

He lowered the barrel of the rifle and I could see that he was momentarily disconcerted. I went on, reckless with angry desperation,

'Suppose I were to just walk on past you? Would you really shoot us? You know you wouldn't! In cold blood? Look. I'm going to visit my sick mother who lives up the road. I'm not doing anything wrong and you're not going to stop me. Now, get out of my way.'

I gripped the boys each by a wrist and stepped forward. For a crazy moment I thought I had won. Then a voice from the other side of the vehicle said quietly,

'Not so fast! Now, just you stand still and hand over your identity cards.'

The second man was older, thicker set than the first. Another local man by his voice, but one accustomed to giving orders. A farmer, perhaps. He came round the bonnet of the

Land Rover so that we were between the two of them and held out his hand. Slowly I drew the identity cards out of my bag and handed them over.

He inspected them in the headlight beam and grunted.

'Thought as much! Knew you weren't local people. Where's your travel permit?'

There was a long second of silence. Tim whimpered.

'I haven't got one.'

The thought crossed my mind 'at least if they arrest us we shall have a roof over our heads—and I suppose they'll feed us'.

'What the 'ell are you doing here then?' he asked sharply. Then went on, 'Never mind that now. You're a job for headquarters, you are. Go on, get in.'

He gestured towards the Landrover. As I moved I said wearily,

'Where's Headquarters?'

'Gloucester,' he answered curtly.

I thought of all the miles we had walked that day. In less than an hour we should be more or less back where we had started. I turned to him.

'Look, I'm telling the truth! I'm going to see my sick mother. She needs me. Can't you let me go?'

He regarded me with a bleak, inexorable patience, as he might have surveyed a late spring frost or a summer drought.

161

'And where might she be, then?'

'In the village.' Once again I was lying at random, with no hope of substantiating my story.

He shook his head and made a movement shepherding us into the vehicle.

'It won't wash, missus. I know everyone hereabouts and I know there's no sick woman with a daughter in Surrey. We've had your likes round here before, trying to sneak over the river. We know what you're up to.'

'But why shouldn't I?' I cried passionately. 'It's not a frontier. Why do you want to stop me?'

'Why do you want to get over there?'

'I've told you—to visit my mother.'

'Oh—I thought she lived just here, in the village.'

I took a long breath, struggling with hysterical tears which had my throat in a grip of steel. It must, somehow, be possible to reason with this man.

'But why shouldn't I travel wherever I like? This is supposed to be a free country and you're trying to turn it into a—a police state.'

'Look 'ere, missus,' he grounded his rifle butt and leaned on it, grasping the muzzle with both hands, 'there's been a sight too much "freedom" in this country, if you ask me. Freedom to strike every time you get a bit fed up, freedom to live off the State if you don't fancy working at all, free sex—freedom to go

162

to the dogs, that's what I call it. Now we've got a Government that wants to pull things together, and I'm behind 'em. I don't know what you've done, or your husband or whatever; but if you hadn't gone against the law somehow you wouldn't be sneaking round the countryside without a travel permit and trying to get across to join people who want to start rebellion and civil war and God knows what. We had another lot like you a week or so back—whole family. Turned out he was some kind of lecturer at University who'd been telling his students to disobey the laws and start riots and demonstrations and so on. Well, he's back where he belongs now; and that's where you're going. So get in and let's have no more argument.'

Tim was sobbing loudly now and Simon was clutching him and staring at the man. I turned and propelled them both towards the car door.

From behind us a man's voice said.

'Hold on a bit, Olly.'

Both our captors swung round. Three men stood across the narrow lane in the beam of the headlights. All were dressed like men who work on the land, in gum boots and duffle coats. I heard a movement to the rear of the Land Rover. Two more men had moved quietly into the road there.

The older of the Civil Militia men said harshly,

'What do you want then, Jim Furniss?'

163

The central figure of the three came a pace or two forward.

'We don't like what you're doing, Olly,' he said, quietly, almost smilingly. 'We know what happened last week and we don't want to see it happen again.'

'You think you're going to stop us then?' The man addressed as Olly spoke with a sneer in his voice.

'I know we are,' Furniss replied quietly.

'Oh yes?'

"Olly" raised his rifle slowly to his shoulder and aimed it at him. I heard the men behind me move forward a quick pace and then the younger Militiaman swung round and levelled his gun at them over the bonnet of the Land Rover. Furniss had not moved.

'Now you get out of my way and back to your farm, Jim Furniss,' Olly said. 'Otherwise I shall have to take this further.'

Furniss put his hands in the pockets of his duffle coat and straddled his legs.

'You're not going anywhere, Olly,' he said, still with the same faint, half contemptuous smile in his voice. 'And you're not going to shoot me, either.'

'What makes you so sure?' Olly asked. There was derision in his voice but I detected a note of unease also. Something told me that these two were old enemies and that Olly had not usually been the victor.

'You've wanted to be top dog around here

all your life, haven't you,' Furniss said. 'Ever since we were kids. But people round here know you too well and they weren't having any. And now some fools who don't know you like we do have put a gun into your hands you think you're going to have it all your own way. Well, I'm here to tell you you're wrong.'

'And I'm telling you to get out of my way,' growled the other man. 'I'm going to count five and then . . .'

Still Furniss did not move.

'You won't shoot, Olly,' he said, 'because for one thing there are five of us and if you did the chances are one of us would have you before you could aim again—and I wouldn't rely too much on that side-kick of yours, either, because he wouldn't have the gumption to pull the trigger, not if you was to order him to. And for another thing—this is where you live, Olly. This is where your land is, so you're stuck with us and we're stuck with you. If you shoot any of us there won't be a soul for miles around here who'll give you the time of day. There won't be a pub as'll serve you, or a man as ll work for you. And it's no good you thinking your KBG pals will look after you because one night there'll be a fire, or one day someone will have an unfortunate accident with a shotgun—and that'll be the end of Oliver Martin. So take your choice, Olly.'

There was a moment of tense silence. On the other side of the Land Rover Oliver

165

Martin's 'side-kick' stirred his feet uneasily and the barrel of the rifle wandered. Olly said,

'Look 'ere. I'm only doing my job and supporting law and order—like what you ought to be doing. You wait till I report back to my headquarters,'

'What'll they do then?' Furniss laughed jeeringly. 'Take reprisals, will they? Decimate the population of the village, will they?'

'They'll put you in jail for assisting criminals to escape, that's what,' snapped Olly.

'Jail, is it?' Furniss's voice had become hard. 'And are you going to "report back" and get me jailed, and then come back and live here? Don't be a fool, man. There's only one thing for you to do. Put down that gun and get on your way, and forget all about what's happened tonight. We'll take care of the woman and the kids. No-one will ever know they've been here. And when this is all over people might—just might—forget how Olly Milton rode round the countryside in his Land Rover trying to terrorize innocent people. Now, are you going to see sense?'

I realized that all through the conversation Furniss had been imperceptibly edging nearer. Olly Milton suddenly realized it too. He had half lowered the rifle as they talked. Now he jerked it up, saying,

'Keep back—I'm warning you . . .'

But as he spoke Furniss leaped forward and seized the barrel of the gun. It went off with a crack that seemed to hit me in the middle of the chest and somewhere close by a man's voice cried out. I seized the boys and flung myself onto the muddy road, trying to push them underneath the Land Rover. Heavy footsteps thudded past our heads. There were shouts and grunts. Then Furniss's voice again, clear and triumphant.

'Right! Now we'll see who's boss. Stand still, both of you. Cliff, is Bob all right?'

Another voice replied, 'Yeah, he's O.K. It's only a scratch.'

Someone bent down and peered under the Land Rover over at us.

'It's all right, you can come out now. There's no danger.'

The boys crawled out but I found myself quite unable to summon up the strength to move. This had been the last straw. I lay still in the mud and sobbed.

Ten minutes later I was in the kitchen of Jim Furniss's farmhouse a short way up the road, wrapped in blankets and sipping scalding tea. He had carried me there as if I had been a child while one of his sons carried Tim and led Simon by the hand. Vaguely I recollected Olly Martin and his companion scrambling into their Land Rover, while someone contemptuously tossed their now-unloaded rifles in after them.

That evening is one of the golden memories of my life. Hot baths and clean, dry nightclothes for all of us; sitting up to a huge farmhouse supper, wrapped in Mrs Furniss's voluminous pink nylon dressing gown; and the kindly, reassuring voices of Jim Furniss and his two sons, Cliff and Terry. And Mrs Furniss apologizing for the fact that she could not offer us coffee or sugar in our tea, while we tucked into bacon and eggs and home-made bread and jam!

Eventually, when I had told my story and Tim had fallen asleep snuggled against me in the angle of the big old settee, I said,

'Is it true that the people on the other side of the river have declared themselves—well, independent?'

He nodded. 'True enough. They've refused to recognize the present Government or to obey the emergency regulations and they won't let anyone across the river without their permission. Bless me if I can see how it's going to end. We've had the army and the air-force patrolling this side for weeks now. I keep expecting them to mount some sort of attack, but they don't seem to be in any hurry. You want to get over there, do you?'

'I was told it might be the best way to get into Wales,' I explained. 'Anyway, right now I just want to get out of the reach of the authorities.'

He leaned towards me.

'What I don't see is what you're supposed to have done wrong. What are you running away for?'

I sighed deeply. 'The ridiculous thing is that I've begun to wonder that myself. Maybe it was all in my imagination—but I really thought that if we stayed at home there was a very good chance of the children being taken away from me and put into care.' I outlined for him my involvement with Jane and my spying activities at the local KBG meetings. 'Now, of course,' I finished, 'I've broken all sorts of regulations and turned us into real outlaws. So I suppose the only thing to do is to go and live with the other outlaws.' I gave him a rueful smile.

He said, 'Oh, they're ordinary enough folk—and law-abiding too. It's just all these new regulations that they don't hold with, and men like Olly Martin being given guns and the right to poke their noses into other people's affairs. And I don't blame them. You'll be all right over there.'

'If I can get across,' I said wearily.

'Oh, don't you worry about that,' he replied, smiling. 'You stay here tonight and tomorrow and lie low. Meanwhile one of my lads will get a message over to the other side, so as they'll be ready for you. We'll get you across tomorrow night—no bother.'

I looked at him. 'You've done this before.'

He grinned. 'Once or twice.' Then he added thoughtfully, 'Pity they know you're in the area, though. I wonder how they found out.'

I asked, 'Did you have a young man, a student, through here—a few days ago? He'd been—badly treated by the police.'

'Oh, yes,' he replied. 'Know him, do you?'

I shook my head. 'No, I was told about him, that's all. Did he—get through all right?'

Jim nodded. 'Yes. Don't you worry. We got him across. It was what he told us made us so mad with Olly Martin for sending those other poor souls back. But, any rate, he's safe enough now.'

Next morning I slept late and woke to a sense of blissful relaxation—like the first morning of a holiday. The sun was shining across my bed and I could hear the voices of Simon and Tim chattering happily with Cliff down in the farm-yard. A few moments later, to complete my euphoria, Mrs Furniss arrived with my breakfast tray.

We spent the whole day relaxing. The boys were happy following Cliff and Terry around the farm, though Jim insisted that they must not leave the yard and the buildings round it. I stayed with Mrs Furniss in the big kitchen, helping her to bake bread.

When it was finished she took out of a cupboard a packet of dried yeast.

'Here,' she said, 'put that in one of your bags. I use fresh yeast mostly but I always keep some of this by for emergencies, like. I don't know how you'll find things over there. I don't suppose they're any worse off than we are, but you might be glad to bake your own bread sometime. Anyway, it's not much to carry.'

I thanked her warmly and put the yeast in my shopping bag. I was learning to value any commodity.

Over the evening meal Jim said,

'We'll leave about eight. It'll be full dark by then. They're expecting you on the other side before midnight. It's about a mile to where the boat is. Are you O.K. to walk it? It's less conspicuous than taking the car.'

I assured him that we were. An hour later we slipped out of the house. Jim leading, followed by Cliff holding Tim by the hand, then myself and Simon, with Terry bringing up the rear. All three men carried shotguns. There was a lot of cloud and no moon. I had forgotten how dark and how vast the countryside can feel when there are no street lamps and no headlights. We moved along the lane in single file, not speaking. I found that I was starting to shiver, although I was warmly clothed, wearing an old sweater of Terry's under my jacket. I looked round at Simon close behind me. His face was solemn, but when I put my hand behind me and found his for a moment it was warm and steady.

It took us about fifteen minutes to reach the river. We passed a cluster of lighted cottages and a pub, strangely dark and silent under the curfew. In the shadow of its wall Jim whispered to us to wait. He and Terry moved

171

off stealthily into the darkness.

'Where have they gone?' I whispered to Cliff.

'Scout around,' he whispered back. 'Wouldn't put it past old Olly Martin to be hanging around somewhere.'

My stomach went cold. Of course, he must guess that we would try to cross the river tonight. It was a perfect opportunity for revenge.

'Suppose he's told the army about us?' I whispered.

'He won't live long, then,' said Cliff laconically.

A distant hum came to my ears, like the buzzing of a big insect.

'What's that?' I asked.

'Patrol boat—on the river,' he replied, 'They go up and down all night, when the choppers can't keep watch.'

The humming grew louder, passed us and faded away. Jim and Terry swiftly crossed the open space of the car park and joined us.

'No sign of anyone,' Jim breathed.

'Good old Olly,' muttered Cliff. 'Knows which side his bread's buttered.'

Jim looked at his watch and said,

'Come on.'

We followed a short track which ended in a slipway. I was surprised and uneasy to see no boat. Then Terry took a torch from his pocket and, pointing it at the opposite bank, flashed it in a rhythmic pattern. As he put it away again he caught my eye and said, half sheepishly,

'I always did like playing smugglers.'

We stood in a huddle under a little group of trees and waited. The silence seemed endless and universal, only enhanced by the slap of water and the ubiquitous rushing of the wind in the trees. Then we heard the patrol boat returning.

Jim muttered, 'Bloody 'ell! They don't usually come back this quick. Here, get down behind these trees, all of you, and keep your faces hidden.'

We crouched in the long wet grass with our heads in our arms. The boat drew closer. Almost opposite us the engine idled and then died. The silence stretched out. Then a voice spoke, indistinctly, from over the water and I was aware of a light from somewhere. I glanced up and had just time to bury my head again before the searchlight beam swept over us.

They stayed about ten minutes, sweeping the bank and the river with the light. Then the engine roared suddenly and hummed away downstream. Slowly, wincing at our cramped limbs, we got to our feet.

'Reckon they were looking for something special?' Terry said, with meaning.

'Shouldn't wonder,' grunted his father.

There was a brief pause, then Cliff said,

'I'll fix that Olly Martin, one day.'

Tim sidled close to me and looked up into my face, whispering,

'What are we waiting for?'

'Any point in hanging on, do you think?' Terry said.

Jim shifted his feet and gazed up and down the river.

'Give it another few minutes.'

'You think the patrol boat has frightened them off?' I murmured.

'Could have done,' he replied. 'For the time being. We may have to wait until tomorrow now.'

'Listen!' whispered Cliff.

After a second or two I distinguished the soft, regular splash of oars. A moment later the dark shape of a rowing boat appeared against the lighter surface of the river. We moved out onto the slipway, hands seized the boat and pulled it in, other hands reached out to help us over the gunwales and before I had time to whisper more than the hastiest thanks and farewells the gap of water was widening between us. The three dark figures on the bank stood watching for a moment, then turned away and disappeared.

There were two men in the boat. Neither spoke except for a low-voiced instruction to keep down in the bow. We huddled there, listening to the surge of water against the side and straining our ears for the hum of the returning patrol boat. On the map the river had not looked particularly wide at this point. Perhaps we were going against the current; anyway, the crossing seemed to take a very long time. I could feel Tim shivering against me.

Then, out of the dark, there was the flash of a torch and once again the soft bump of the boat against the side and more hands reaching out to help us ashore. A few hasty, reassuring words, a walk of a few paces and we saw a pony and trap awaiting us. The muffled figure holding the reins turned as we climbed in and a woman's voice said,

'That's right, love. In you get. You'll be all right with us.'

Florrie Evans, large, cheerful and forthright, was our guide and hostess for the next day or so. From her I learned how anti-government demonstrations had grown into several days of street fighting in towns like Ross and Monmouth before the civil authorities and the police had declared themselves on the side of the demonstrators and the new Civil Militia and other KBG supporters had been forced to lie low or flee across the river. There had been one rather half-hearted attempt by government forces to cross the river and re-establish authority, fiercely resisted by the local population. Now they waited, puzzled by the apparent inactivity of the army. Remembering Clare's account of the state of affairs in the country as a whole I was able to

175

supply the answer.

The next day Florrie's pony and trap took us to the old Speeche House in the centre of the Forest of Dean which had once been the meeting place of the foresters' court. A hotel more recently, it now housed the men who were in charge of this rebellious territory, which was so much more peaceful than the areas I had recently passed through.

Here I was interviewed by an oddly assorted group which clearly involved several factions. They listened closely to my story but many of the questions were pointed, some overtly hostile. I became aware of the rank smell of my own fear as I realized that some of them suspected me of being a spy.

Finally they appeared to be satisfied with my answers and the meeting broke up. The man who had chaired it and who appeared to be in a position of some authority, although he never identified himself, offered me a cup of tea, which turned out to be a strange herbal brew. Real tea, it appeared, was unobtainable in Ross. As I sipped it he apologized for the harshness of some of the questioning.

'You have to understand, Mrs Fairing, that this is a case of necessity making very odd bedfellows. Since our—defiance—of the authorities has been known a number of very strange people have come to us with offers of help. We need them, but at the same time many of us are not prepared to go to the sort of lengths which they are advocating.'

'Do you mean the IRA?' I asked.

He nodded, giving me a shrewd look. 'And others.'

I told him about Reading. He sighed and sipped his tea.

'It was to be expected, of course. A good many people will be only too happy to fish in these troubled waters. Part of our problem is to discover the exact source of these offers of help. If we knew for certain it might persuade some of our more impulsive friends to look at them a little more sceptically. However,' he looked up and smiled at me briefly, 'I think you may have helped us to avert one very extreme course of action.'

'What was that?' I asked.

'The suggestion has been made,' he said quietly, 'that we should embark on a campaign of sabotage, beginning by blowing up the Severn Road Bridge. Our so-called friends say they can supply the explosives and the technical expertise, and some of our own people were very much in favour. However, if we can convince them that there is no immediate danger of the army moving in here the whole idea becomes, well, at least less urgent. And if the Government is, as you suggest, on the verge of collapse, the enterprise is pointless.' He smiled and rose. 'Your news has given me more hope than any I've had for some days, Mrs Fairing.'

Seeing that the interview was coming to an end I took the opportunity to raise the question of my own journey. He compressed his lips and shook his head.

'I really think that it would be a trifle foolhardy to insist on continuing, Mrs Fairing. Why not stay here for the time being? After all, it may not be so much longer. There are a number of local people who have expressed their willingness to take in refugees like yourself, and the schools are still open. You would be able to live without any fear of reprisals or any harassment from the authorities. What do you say?'

I wrestled with the new idea. The prospect of travelling no further was certainly attractive, but nonetheless we should be among strangers. I thought of my parents, who must already be worried by the lack of news from me. The foetal instinct was still strong. I needed to be with them. I said,

'No, thank you for the offer, but I must get to my parents if I possibly can. They'll be worried.'

He looked at me for a moment and sighed.

'I admire your courage, but I'm afraid there isn't a great deal I can do to help. However, I'll make some enquiries. There may be someone going north from here who could take you part of the way. See my secretary tomorrow.' He offered me his hand, and added, 'If you find that you have to give up the idea, or you run into any trouble, don't hesitate to come and see me again. It distresses me more than I can say to see innocent people like yourself being hounded around the country. Emerson and his crew will have a lot to account for when the time comes.'

He was not the only one to try and dissuade us from continuing our journey but by mid-morning the following day we were wedged into the cab of a farm truck with a large taciturn farmer from Hay-on-Wye who had come into Ross with his produce because the siege economy offered higher prices than the government stronghold of Hereford. The truck ground along up the Golden Valley, serene and untroubled as its name suggested under the shadow of the Black Mountains. With the cross-questioning of the previous day behind me I was glad of the farmer's silence and the boys were somnolent in the warm cab. My mood, which swung with increasing violence from anxiety and despair to euphoric optimism as each day passed, had reached another crest. We were on our way again. I did not doubt, just then, that we should find someone to take us on our journey once we reached Hay.

My high spirits were abruptly deflated when we reached the farmer's home. In a few monosyllabic answers he affirmed that he knew no-one who might take us further nor could he suggest anyone to whom we might safely apply. His tone implied that what we did and where we went next was no concern of his. I divined that he had taken my drowsy silence for haughtiness and that now my protestations of gratitude came too late. An offer of money 'towards the petrol' was accepted but produced no further assistance. Within minutes we were standing on the road, our two pathetic bags at our feet. I looked at the boys. They looked back at me, doggedly expectant. In that moment, more so than when we had sat in the growing darkness outside Philip Woodstock's church, more even than when we had faced Oliver Martin with his rifle, I came close to panic and despair.

I picked up the bags and we set off down the lane, following the course of the river, the broad valley green and still in the sunshine. After four or five miles we came to an ancient toll bridge, hump-backed and too narrow to take two cars at once. There were no guards. As we passed a woman looked out from the little window where the tolls were collected, but she only nodded to us with a kind of vague politeness.

We left the main road for a lane which ran northwards and here we sat down on the grass verge and I took out my AA book, which was the only map I had for this area. My finger traced a route. Kington, Presteigne, Knighton—then where? Newtown, then on into the mountains. It must be—how far? Fifty miles? Sixty, perhaps. If we walked ten miles a day for six days . . . Was I mad? What had possessed me to leave the Forest? I looked at the boys. Already Tim was complaining about being tired. And what about food? All I had in my bag were three Cornish pasties and a bottle of milk given to me by my hostess of the night before, and it was already past lunch time. I got the food out and watched their faces brighten. But where did the next meal come from? And where did we sleep tonight?

Horse hooves sounded from around the bend. A young man appeared, leading a sturdily built brown horse. He was as thick-set and sturdy as the animal, but there was something about the way he led it, keeping well ahead of it with the full length of the rope between them, that suggested to me that he was not used to handling horses. When he saw us he half checked his stride, as if surprised and disconcerted. Then he walked on, dropping his head and looking sideways at us. I had the impression that he was inclined to stop and speak, but he obviously thought better of it.

As he was about to pass, I spoke on impulse. 'Excuse me . . .'

He stopped sharply and looked at me.

'Yeah?'

'I was wondering if you could help us . . .' I rose and went nearer to him. 'Do you know any way we might get transport into Kington, or even further on, if possible?'

He looked from me to the children. When he spoke, it was with the accent of urban Birmingham, strangely out of place in this setting.

'Travelling far, are you?'

'I'm hoping to get to Dolgelly.' If this turned out to be a KBG supporter, it was just too bad. I was too tired to weigh the possibilities any more.

He sucked his lips. 'That's a fair step, that is. On foot, are you? You'll never make it.'

'We're hoping to get a lift—or something.'

He shook his head. 'Not much chance of that. What with petrol rationing and travel permits and that people aren't going far.' He continued to scrutinize us. 'Live round here, do you?'

'No,' I said flatly, and met his eyes.

'Look,' he went on after another pause, 'I'm—sharing a house, with some mates of mine near here. If you've nowhere to stop you'd be welcome. Maybe one of them could think of something.'

I hesitated. I was certain he had guessed our predicament. Was this a genuine offer of help, or a trap? I had only my instinct to go on.

'That's very kind of you,' I said. 'We certainly could do with a bed for the night. If you're sure there would be room for us.'

'Oh, no problem there,' he said. 'Great big rambling old place it is. Come on then. It's about three miles from here.'

'Come on, boys,' I said, and they scrambled unwillingly to their feet.

The young man looked at them.

'Would you like to ride on the horse?'

'Yes, *please*,' they said with one voice.

I held the halter rope while he lifted them up, one behind the other. Their faces had broken into delighted grins. He turned, grinning too, and took the rope from me.

'My name's Barney, by the way,' he said, and added, jerking his head at the horse, 'I don't know what he's called. We've only just met, and he doesn't talk much.'

CHAPTER FIVE

IDYLL

The farm stood at the head of a shallow valley, the hills rising steep behind it but the land in front sloping away more gently towards the now distant Wye. There was a sprawl of grey stone buildings, not pretty but solidly determined to ignore the rotting window frames and other evidences of long neglect. By the creaking iron gate which barred the lane a faded and drunkenly angled sign bore the name 'Brynwcws'.

'That means "Mount of Health" in Welsh,'

Barney said, leading the horse through while I held the gate open. 'Least, that's what they say. I wouldn't know myself.'

'Are you sure it will be all right for us to stay here?' I asked, voicing the anxiety I had stifled while we plodded up the lane. 'I mean, who does it belong to?'

He grinned. 'Nobody, I reckon. Not now. Don't worry, it'll be all right.'

As the horse clopped into the yard a door opened and a young man came out. Seeing us, he stood for a second, one hand resting on the door post, looking us over. He was dressed in jeans cut off above the knee, a tattered shirt open to the waist and sandals. His dark hair was long, lying thickly on the back of his neck, and his skin wherever it was visible was deeply tanned.

Barney said, 'I found them down on the main road. They've got nowhere to go.'

The young man moved forward. He carried himself very erect, like a dancer, so that I was surprised when he came up to me to find that he was only a few inches taller than I was. His eyes were very large, hazel in colour, and defined by a line of thick dark lashes. He extended his hand.

'Hallo. I'm Hal. Welcome to Brynwcws.' The voice was carefully classless but unmistakably cultured. The hand clasp was warm and firm.

'My name's Nell Fairing,' I said. How many

184

times had I been through all this in the last week? 'These are my children, Simon and Tim.'

Barney had helped the boys down off the horse and they stood close to me on either side.

Hal said, 'Come on in. I expect you're tired.'

The farm kitchen was long and low, with a stone floor and massive wooden beams. The deal table in the centre was littered with what I assumed was the remains of lunch for several people and the primitive sink in one corner was stacked with dirty dishes and pans. Muddy wellingtons and discarded coats lay about. Hal cleared three chairs, displacing a pile of books, a guitar and a sleepy tabby cat, and we sat down.

An interior door opened and an amazingly beautiful girl drifted through it. Part of her long fair hair was plaited and twisted around her head to hold the rest in place and she wore a long soft cotton skirt in subtle colourings which could only have come from India and a peasant blouse with wide loose sleeves. She could have stepped straight off the pages of a book of fairy tales, or the pavement of King's Road, Chelsea. Huge violet blue eyes, wide open like a doll's so that the lids disappeared completely, gazed at us in mild surprise.

Hal said, 'This is Jinny. Love, do you know where the boys are?'

She transferred her gaze to him and said

softly,

'I'll go and get them.'

When the door closed behind her there was a silence. Barney had gone off with the horse. Hal drew up a chair, sat down astride it, leaned on the back and gave me a slow smile; but he said nothing.

'Are there many of you here?' I asked at length.

'Six,' he replied. 'You'll meet the others in a minute—except for Old Bill. He's out in his garden. We shan't see him till dark.'

'Do you live here?' I was not sure how to phrase my inquiries without offence.

He nodded with the same slow smile. 'At the moment. I expect I'll stay. I don't know about the others.'

The door opened again and Jinny returned followed by two more young men. Hal said,

'Meet Alexis and Paul.' This is Neil, and these are Simon and Tim.'

Jinny drifted over to the window and sat on the deep sill, leaning her head against the wall. The two men stood together a moment in the doorway, murmuring conventional greetings. Then Alexis, the older of the two, came forward.

'Have you come far?'

It was a relief, after Hal's silent acceptance, to be questioned. I began to tell my story. While I did so Paul moved quietly to a big larder leading off the kitchen and came back with a jug of milk. He took three glasses from the table and rinsed them at the sink before setting one in front of each of us. The milk tasted good.

When I had finished my tale there was another silence. I had grown used to being eagerly questioned and cross-questioned and was surprised by my new hosts' apparent lack of curiosity.

Hal said, 'You're welcome to stay here, as long as you like. But I'm afraid we can't get you any further.'

I sighed wearily. 'I don't see how we are ever going to get there unless we can get hold of a car and some petrol.'

'Not much chance of that, I'm afraid,' Alexis said. 'That's why we want the horse.'

'Just a minute,' Paul put in, speaking for the first time. 'Couldn't they come with us?'

Alexis looked at him sharply and then at us.

'I don't know. I don't think there would be room.'

Paul perched on the edge of the table.

'We're actors, you see. That is, Alexis and I and Jinny. We tour round with our own show. We've been here for the winter but we'll be off again soon. I'm sure we could squeeze you in somehow.' He was fair haired, slender and loose limbed as a colt, with a wide mobile mouth and lively eyes half hidden under thick, sandy lashes. I guessed he could not be much more than twenty. He lifted his head and looked at the older man. 'Come on, Lexi, you know we could.'

Alexis turned to look at him. He had what, to me, was the typical actor's face; long, straight nose, high cheek bones, strong arched eyebrows above hooded eyes, lines beginning to be etched about the eyes and from the wide nostrils to the corners of the lips. As he looked at Paul I saw a flicker of movement about his mouth that suggested some inner conflict. Then he said,

'There won't be any show to take out if we don't get on. We're supposed to be rehearsing, remember?' He turned to the door and then glanced back at me. 'Excuse us.'

He went out. Paul said, 'See you later,' and followed him and Jinny rose in silence and trailed after them both.

I looked at Hal. He grinned.

'I'm afraid they live in a world of their own, like most actors.'

'What about you?' I asked. 'You don't belong here, either. Do you?'

He stretched his arms and then relaxed again.

'While I'm here I do. It's O.K. I like it here.'

'But what do you do?' I persisted. 'How do you come to be here in the first place?'

Tim had got up and gone to the window.

'Can we go outside and look round, Mum?'

'Is that all right?' I said to Hal.

He nodded. 'Sure. Go where you like.

Barney'll be out there somewhere.'

The boys slipped out into the yard. I returned my attention to Hal.

'I'm sorry if I'm asking too many questions, but I can't help being curious.'

'Fair enough,' he replied. 'You've told us your story.'

He got up and went to lean in the doorway which the boys had left open, his back against the door post. For a moment he looked out, then he turned his head back to me.

'I came here last summer. I'd been up for a free festival on top of Cader Idris.' He nodded towards the guitar. 'I sing, see. Afterwards I was hitching back towards London, just bumming along you know, and I was right out of bread. I asked a bloke in the village for a job. He told me the old man up here might want a hand. He was a rum old devil. Hated people. Lived all by himself up here, never went off the place unless he had to. But he'd got to the stage where he couldn't manage any longer on his own. We got along O.K. Doesn't bother me if a bloke doesn't speak all day. He was no fool, though. He'd got ideas. That's one of them, out there.'

He nodded to something beyond the range of my vision. I got up and went to the door. Beyond the grey humps of barns and outhouses a sloping field was seamed with neat rows of low green bushes.

'Know what those are?' Hal asked.

189

I shook my head.

'Vines,' he said. 'That's a south facing slope. Ideal position. The old man put them in four years ago. Last autumn we made our first vintage. He never lived to taste it, poor old sod. They were the only thing he really cared about, those vines.'

'But surely you can't grow wine here?' I said.

'Why not?' He looked at me. 'The Romans did. They're making wine already in other parts of South Wales—good wine, too.'

'Did you say the old man was dead?' I pursued, picking up another thread from his story.

He nodded. 'About a month ago. Caught a bad cold, wouldn't stay in bed. Obstinate old devil, he was. One morning he didn't get up. When I went to look he was in a bad way. Only lasted a couple of hours longer.'

'Couldn't you get him into hospital, or get a doctor or something?' I asked.

He shrugged and shook his head. 'He wouldn't have wanted it. He'd rather have died here, in his own bed.'

'But if he's dead,' I said slowly, 'how is it you're still here?'

He looked at me, the large dark eyes brooding on my face.

'Why not? He didn't have any children. No-one wants the farm. If I went who'd look after it?'

'But who owns it now? Surely there must have been a will, some sort of legal . . . arrangements . . .' I felt completely lost.

He smiled the slow smile. 'Legally, the old man's still alive.'

'You mean you never told anyone?'

He moved past me, back to his chair and sat down.

'Look. By the time he died this government was in. O.K? That meant identity cards, direction of labour, all that hassle. I don't have an identity card, I don't have a permanent address. With the old man dead I don't have a job or a home. We buried him in the orchard. He never went near anyone if he could help it. No-one will miss him.'

I sat down on the window seat and stared at him.

'So you're just squatting here.'

He spread his hands. 'You could call it that.'

'But how do you manage? I mean what about food—ration books and so on?'

'We manage. There are two cows, and some chickens. Last summer the old man had all the wheat we harvested ground into flour and stored away in the barn. He could see what was coming. Then we killed a pig before Christmas. He knew about preserving hams and all that stuff. And we have vegetables. Old Bill sees to them. And I still have the old man's ration book, of course. We get a bit on that—sugar and things, when there's any

191

about. They're used to me getting his stuff for him down in the village and they don't ask questions.'

'Just a minute,' I exclaimed. 'Who's Old Bill?'

He laughed softly at my confusion. 'He's an old fellow who turned up here a couple of months ago. He came down from Manchester. Used to work in the cotton mills. He's been unemployed for three years, so he set off south, looking for work. I don't know how he ended up here but he came trudging up the lane asking if we had any odd jobs. He's as happy as a sandboy out there with his veges. His allotment was the only thing that made life in Manchester bearable, he reckons.'

'So,' I said slowly, sorting out what I had heard, 'That's the six of you. Old Bill and the three actors and Barney—and you.'

'That's right.' He grinned. 'And now there's you and the two kids.'

'But can we all . . . manage here?' I asked. 'I mean, can the farm feed us all?'

'Have you got ration books?' he asked suddenly.

'Yes,' I said, 'but I daren't show them to anyone. We've no permit to be so far from home.'

'Oh, you don't want to worry about that,' he replied. 'I told you. They don't ask questions in the village. I'll take your books in along with the old man's and the woman in the shop will give us what she can.' He got up and then, seeing my anxious look, stopped and smiled down at me. 'No problem. Honestly. You'll be O.K. here. Come on, I'll find you a room.'

The next morning I came downstairs to find the stack of dirty dishes in the kitchen roughly the same size as it had been yesterday. Apparently the normal routine was only to wash something when you could find nothing else to use instead. At one end of the littered table Jinny was desultorily kneading a grey-looking mass in a basin.

'Good morning.' I said. 'Baking?'

She poked the unyielding dough gloomily. 'It's supposed to be bread, but I don't know how to make it properly. Just because I'm a woman . . .'

'Have you got any yeast?' I asked.

She looked at me, pushing back a long curtain of pale hair which she had not yet bound up.

'Yeast? No.'

One of the sudden flushes of happiness which were becoming a familiar part of my repeated emotional cycle swept over me. I went to the bag I had brought with me and rummaged in it.

'There!' I said triumphantly, producing Mrs Furniss's packet of dried yeast.

Jinny put the back of her hand across her face, leaving a white smudge of flour.

'What do I do with it?'

193

I laughed. 'Leave it to me, Jinny. I'll see to it. I expect you've got some rehearsing to do, haven't you?'

Her face brightened like a child let off a disagreeable chore.

'Oh great! Thanks Nell. You're super!'

A moment later she was gone.

I turned the unappetizing mess out of the bowl and started again. Then, while the dough proved, I started on the kitchen. There was no running hot water but the big range was alight. With a zest I had not felt for months I boiled up water, and scoured dishes and pans. When I had finished with them I attacked the kitchen table, the thick grease on the top of the range, and finally the floor.

By the time I had finished the smell of fresh bread was stealing out of the oven. I washed my hands and poured myself a glass of milk— preferable to the ersatz coffee. In the bottom of my bag there was still half a jar of jam, and someone apparently knew how to make butter for there was a dish in the larder. Ten minutes later I was sitting relaxed at the table eating fresh rolls and listening to Simon and Tim shouting somewhere outside when Hal came in. He stopped in the doorway and gazed round.

'Hey! What's happened here?'

I smiled at him.

'It's called cleaning up. It's an improvement, don't you think?'

194

He came over to the table. 'It's great. But are you sure you wanted to do it?'

I laughed. 'I enjoyed it—really!'

He looked relieved. 'That's all right then. Hey man! That looks like real bread!'

'The edible kind,' I agreed. 'I just made it.'

He seized a roll and a knife and began to spread butter thickly. Then he saw the jar.

'Jam? I haven't seen jam in months!'

With his mouth full of roll he ran to the door and shouted,

'Barney! Alex! Everyone—come here!'

Within minutes they descended on the kitchen and fell on the bread with cries of delight. I watched them demolish at one sitting nearly half my baking and all the jam. I could only make sure that Simon and Tim got their share. Everyone was full of compliments; there was a lot of laughter and warm cameraderie; but when they finally drifted off again the table was littered with crumbs and dirty plates. Slowly I got up and put another kettle on the range.

When the kitchen was straight again I wandered out into the yard. The weather was beginning to settle into the pattern of one of the finest, warmest springs for years and the sun caressed my face. I could hear a blue tit's insistent, piercing double note from the patch of woodland below the farm. Lambs bleated up on the hills. I wondered if they belonged to the farm too.

195

The days slipped past. I wandered the farm, talking, listening, watching, slowly beginning to piece together the jig-saw of different stories, different backgrounds, and fit them into the present routine of the farm. Routine was hardly the word, for there was no formal pattern, no precise division of responsibility. Each did, in the current language, his own thing. Barney, the Birmingham factory worker who had abandoned his home to escape the fighting and the imminent threat of starvation, cared for the animals and declared that, whatever happened, he was never going back to the production line. Old Bill disappeared immediately after breakfast to his vegetable patch. I watched his small wiry form tirelessly digging and hoeing, his stubby fingers weeding and planting. At work he was taciturn, inclined to be grumpy. In the evenings he would sit sucking his empty pipe by the range and could sometimes be persuaded to talk of his past life.

It was a life which bitterly encompassed the worst of our century; a father killed in the First War; a working life begun in the depression; service in the Second War; a couple of decades of prosperity, then unemployment and a steady decline in living standards and his own self-esteem. His wife had died two years back. His children had emigrated. To spend his days pursuing his hobby, which at the same time made him useful to this community, however alien, was a kind of happiness.

Hal worked around the farm when the mood took him. Certain jobs, like keeping the kitchen range alight, he did as a matter of habit and he would sometimes work for hours among the young vines on the hill but he had no overall plan for the farm as a whole. No land was ploughed, no grain planted. I began to see that when the natural resources he had, in a manner of speaking, inherited ran out he would simply move on. When he was not working he would sit in the sun and strum his guitar or talk lengthily, discursively, to anyone who was free to listen. At such times he had a quietude, a quality of repose, that drew me strongly. I found myself seeking his company, enjoying the slow smile, the gentle brooding of his dark eyes; enjoying too the sight of the thick dark locks on the back of his neck and his poised, graceful movements. I noticed that, in spite of his unkempt appearance, he was always scrupulously clean.

I learned that he had dropped out of his second year at Oxford. He had spent a year wandering round Europe, coming to rest for a while in Greece; then returned to try and make a living from the songs which he wrote and sung. They were ironic, quirky, clever lyrics with complex melodies, haunting yet hard to remember. I could see why he had never penetrated further than the fringes of the pop world. Yet until last summer those fringes had supported him, together with unemployment benefit and the occasional odd job. He was twenty-four.

The three actors were the most intriguing and mysterious of the group to me. Exquisite, self-absorbed, they wandered about the house, exercising, arguing, sometimes loudly high-spirited, sometimes moody and depressed, Alexis was the dominant character. It had been his theory that the chronic lack of employment for actors could only be solved by taking theatre to the people. Accordingly they had pooled their resources to buy a caravan and had spent the previous summer touring Wales, setting up on village greens and in pub forecourts and passing round the hat afterwards. Their last show of the summer had been in Hay. It was there that Hal had seen them and had persuaded the old farmer to give them winter accommodation on the farm.

The show was a mixture of scenes and sketches, with dance and mime and a bit of Shakespeare for good measure. Now they were trying to devise something more coherent, 'more relevant to the time we are living in', in Alexis' phrase. Occasionally I was allowed to watch them rehearse and was amazed by their sheer expertise, by the intensity of imagination which possessed them. The girl, Jinny, fascinated me. Normally she was little more than a lovely shadow, drifting among us, enfolding in herself her own mysterious joys and sorrows. When she began to act it was as if she began only then to exist. A vibrant depth of emotion glowed in her and an intense sexuality which affected even me. Once I said to Hal,

'Is Jinny Paul's girl friend, or Alexis? I can never make out.'

He looked up with his slow grin and said,

'Neither.'

'Do you mean to say that they manage to live and work together without any sort of sexual involvement? I don't see how any man could ignore Jinny.'

He cocked his head sideways.

'Aw, come on, Nell. You're not that naive. Alexis and Paul aren't interested in Jinny because they're only interested in each other.'

I blinked and another piece of jig-saw fell into place.

'Of course, how stupid of me. It's obvious when you think about it. I suppose I'm not used to looking for that sort of thing.'

We were sitting on the doorstep, catching the last of the sun. Hal was mending an old harness he had found in the barn. He was neat and clever with his fingers, infinitely patient with jobs I would have given up as hopeless in a few minutes. The harness was for Bruno, as we had named the horse. Barney had collected him from a riding school which could no longer afford to feed him and the theory was that he should pull the ramshackle caravan which was the three actors' travelling home, now that there was no more petrol for Alexis' car. The caravan stood in the yard, its sides adorned with bold, gaudy, rather childlike pictures of Harlequin, Columbine and Pantaloon. The makeshift shafts which Barney and Hal had constructed stuck out oddly from a body designed for a different form of motive power and I had grave doubts about Bruno's reactions to it, but no-one else seemed to be worried.

After a moment I went on.

'But if that's so, why is Jinny with them? I mean, I should have thought a girl like that would have wanted to be the centre of male attention.'

Hal stopped working on the harness and leaned his head back on the door post.

'It's not so surprising really. I've met girls like Jinny before. They look like sex goddesses but you touch them once and they run for cover.'

'And Jinny's like that?'

'You ask Barney!'

'Not you?'

He grinned wryly. 'Like the man said, once bitten, twice shy.'

'But why should Jinny be like that? Do you mean she's afraid of sex?'

'She wouldn't admit it, of course. Her story is that she's in love with one of the tutors at her old college—a married man, naturally. The fact is, she only feels safe near a man who is unobtainable. That's why she's happy with Paul and Alexis. And it suits Alexis very well because the only thing in this world that frightens him is the thought that Paul might go off with someone else.'

He looked up and caught my eye. I found myself smiling at him. He said quietly,

'You're more of a woman than Jinny, and always will be; but of course you know that.'

I looked away, feeling an absurd glow of satisfaction. We were close together on the step. I could feel the warmth of his body. I moved slightly, relaxed. My arm touched his. His skin was smooth and sun-warmed. He took my hand for a moment and put it against his cheek. Inside the house Tim called me. I got up quickly and went indoors.

Those days were not, however, free from tensions. I had flung myself with a kind of relish into the domestic routine of cleaning and cooking because it was familiar, a necessary part of my programme of life. If I had thought that the force of my example would change the attitude of the others I was wrong. It rapidly became clear that in their minds I had cast myself in the role of house-mother and they were quite happy to accept me as such, as long as it did not affect their way of life. To begin with I prepared meals and washed up in uncomplaining self-sacrifice which rapidly developed into a growing sense of martyrdom, while I waited for someone to

201

offer to help. No-one did. Then I began to drop broad hints. These fell on deaf ears or were treated as a joke. Finally I began my own policy of direction of labour.

I started with Jinny, despising myself for lacking the courage to tackle one of the men first.

'Would you help me wash up, please, Jinny?'

She never refused, but I had to repeat the request after every meal and after the first time or two she would rise with a heavy sigh and a look of appeal towards Alexis. He, however, refused to come to her rescue. When I attempted to conscript Paul it was a different story. They had work to do, suddenly.

One evening I determined to have it out with all of them, once and for all.

'Listen everyone,' I said, my voice self-consciously loud in the quiet room. 'I think we ought to have a talk about—well, about the way we do things, while we are all living here.'

They looked at me a moment in silence then Hal rose and pulled out a chair at the head of the table.

'O.K. Nell. Everyone's entitled to say what they want to say. You carry on.'

Awkwardly I seated myself in the chair. Old Bill took out his empty pipe and began to suck on it.

'Well, it's just that I feel we ought to have a bit of—organization. After all, there are a lot of us and it would be easier if—well, if everyone knew what was expected of him or her—if everyone had their own jobs.'

'I've got my job,' Barney said. 'The animals aren't complaining.'

'Oh, I know Barney,' I said quickly. 'You work pretty hard, but there are lots of other things—people—could do to make things easier.'

Alexis rose.

'I'm sorry, but if this is going to turn into a discussion of the relative value to society of workers like Barney and artists like us, I don't want to take part in it. Excuse me.'

'That's not what I'm trying to say at all!' I exclaimed.

He looked at me, lifting the arched, expressive eyebrows.

'Isn't it? Forgive me, Nell, but I think you're suffering from the Martha and Mary syndrome—with heavy leanings towards Martha.'

'Just a minute,' Hal put in quietly. 'Give Nell a chance, Alexis. She's got a right to a hearing.'

Alexis shrugged and sat down again. I had the impression that from being chairman of the inquiry I had become prisoner in the dock.

'Look, all I'm trying to say . . .' I could feel my throat beginning to tighten with emotion. 'Ever since we came here I've done my best to keep the place clean and get proper meals and see that we don't waste food. And no-one has lifted a finger to help me, or even said "thank you". Well, I'm getting fed up with being your skivvy, so either we have some arrangement for sharing the work or you can all go back to living like pigs, as you were doing before I came.' I was furious to hear the crack in my voice, feel the prick of tears behind my eyes.

Hal said quietly, 'No-one asked you to do it, Nell. You said you wanted to.'

'That's right!" I shouted at him. 'That's all the gratitude I get. You've been glad enough to eat the food I've cooked . . .' It was all going wrong, sounding like some dreadful travesty of a domestic drama.

'Sure we're glad,' he cut in, rising and coming to stand near me. 'You're a great cook and we enjoy the food—but not if you're going to be miserable making it. If you don't want to do it, you don't have to.'

'And who will do it then, if I don't?'

He lifted his shoulders. 'We managed before. We just got what we wanted when we felt like it.'

I was beginning to tremble. 'That's typical of you! Do what you like, when you like. Never mind anyone else. Never tackle anything the least bit arduous or unpleasant. Your whole life's a mess, no wonder you're happy living in one!'

'The world's a mess, Nell,' he answered, sober but unruffled.

'And your answer is to run away and hide!' I

204

snapped. 'You can't complain about society being in a mess. You can't even make it work here on this farm. Not one of you has thought about what's going to happen in the next few months, even here. Nobody has planted wheat, or bought another pig or tried to raise chickens. What happens if we're all here in six months' time?'

'Speaking for ourselves, we never intended to stay for more than the winter,' Alexis remarked stiffly.

'And what about the rest of us?' I screamed at him. 'You're so selfish, so self-absorbed—all of you . . .' I could not hide my tears any longer but sat with my hand over my eyes, feeling them drip from my fingers onto the table.

Hall took me by the shoulders. Unwillingly I looked up at him.

'Listen Nell. I guess you've been used to a pretty structured environment—get up at a certain time, meals at regular hours, do your work, keep the place clean and so on. But you've got to accept that people don't have to live like that. It's one of the things that I wanted to get away from. Some people like to live in little boxes because it makes them feel safe. Some of us want to be a bit more free. Now, if you need that sort of life, that's great by us. You can clean and cook and do all these other things, but it's because you want to do them—need to do them. We enjoy the results, but we can manage without. Now, if any time you don't want to make a meal—just don't make it. No-one's going to complain. If you don't want to wash up—don't. We'll wash when we need to. Only don't try to make rules, because rules mean authority, and people giving orders and others being punished for not obeying and we're just not into all that. Understand? You do your thing and we'll do ours. No hassle. O.K. ?'

I swallowed and turned my head away. He let me go and went out into the yard. After a moment I got up and went to my room.

The next day I left the house uncleaned and prepared no lunch. People drifted in and helped themselves to hunks of cheese and glasses of milk. No-one commented. The used plates and glasses were left on the table. I went out and sat in the sun in the yard. The time dragged. After a while I got up and went inside to clear up.

Hal came in. He had a long, long daisy chain looped across his hands. I had seen him in the orchard with the two boys busy with it. As I turned from the sink he came and hung it around my neck. Sunlight struck sideways from the window across his face, giving the dark hair an edge of amber. As I smiled and murmured 'Thanks' he leaned and kissed me gently. We stood together. I could feel his slender, compact body lightly against my own but he did not hold me and when I drew back he smiled briefly into my eyes and went away again.

That evening, sitting by the table while he sang softly to his guitar, I repeated to myself 'He's twenty-four. He's a boy. You're thirty-six. Compared to him you're a middle aged woman.' It didn't stop me watching him, hoping to catch his eye, looking for a smile and thrilling secretly when I received one.

Hal went once a week to the little village store to get what he could in the way of supplies. On the evening after his next visit he suddenly exclaimed,

'Does anyone know what tomorrow is?'

We looked at him curiously.

'What?'

'Good Friday. I happened to overhear the woman reminding someone the shop would be shut.'

There was a general murmur of exclamation and comment. I sat silent. We had been at the farm nearly three weeks. It was almost four since we had left home. I tried not to think of my parents' puzzlement and anxiety. Perhaps they had put my long silence down to the general breakdown in communications. What was going on now in the rest of the country? We had no radio and saw no papers, not that either had contained much useful information recently. Hal deliberately never talked politics when he went to the village. He said it was safer not to. Local gossip tended to confine itself to local affairs and a stranger asking questions would be regarded with suspicion. I suspected that he actually wanted to cut himself off from what was happening. Brynwcws was his world and he wanted it intact, undisturbed.

'Anyway,' Hal went on, 'I reckon we ought to do something—on Saturday night, say.'

'What sort of something?' Paul asked.

'Have a party. After all, Easter was a pagan fertility festival long before Christ. Here we are, living close to Nature like this—I think we ought to celebrate the coming of Spring.'

It was agreed with alacrity. I set to work to produce what I could in the way of party food. Jinny decorated the kitchen with great bunches of wild daffodils and Alexis offered the use of the cassette player which was normally jealously guarded to preserve its batteries, as it provided the music for their show. As his contribution Hal announced that it was time to taste the first vintage from the Brynwcws vines.

He had persuaded Alexis that this evening would be a suitable time to try out their new show. That was to be given before supper. Then we would ceremonially broach the first barrel of wine. After that we would eat and then there would be music and dancing.

By late afternoon we were all seated along the wall of the farmhouse facing a stage made from collapsible rostra and backed by the caravan. Alexis, Paul and Jinny had disappeared inside the van half an hour earlier. The last rays of the sun struck the stage like a spotlight. Then the music started and three vivid, exotic figures leaped onto the stage. I had always assumed that a large part of the magic of the theatre was due to clever scenery and effective lighting, the spectator sitting in the darkened auditorium watching distant but vividly illuminated figures. This was a totally different experience. Against their ramshackle background the three actors had recreated the old world of the Commedia del Arte. (Paul had given me a long lecture on the tradition behind this technique which I had only half understood at the time.) Though they used the old figures of Harlequin, Pierrot and Columbine the effect was immediate and striking and we soon found ourselves not only emotionally but physically involved. Much of the programme was pure entertainment but there were also items of bitter satire which struck directly at the government. They made me tremble for the group's future safety but they certainly went down well with the present audience. When the show ended the cheers and shouts would have done credit to Covent Garden or the last night of the Proms.

Then came the great moment of tasting the new wine. I held my breath as Hal drew off the first jugful, praying that for his sake it would be drinkable. Ceremonially everyone was given a glass, even the boys. Hal jumped up on a chair and we waited expectantly.

'My friends,' he cried, 'tonight is dedicated to Dionysus, God of the theatre and of wine. May he inspire us all!'

He raised his glass and downed the contents at a gulp. Around me the others repeated the toast and drank too. I sipped cautiously. The wine was very light, rather acid but beneath the sharp, slightly prickly first taste there was the undeniable aroma of the grape. I drank some more and was aware of Hal beside me. He was laughing, exultant.

'And Nell is our Ceres, our Earth Mother— Queen of the Feast!'

The memory of the evening dissolves into a warm blur of food and music and laughter. Whatever the wine may have lacked to the palate of a gourmet it was certainly high in alcohol and like most inferior wines, improved in proportion to the amount drunk. When we had eaten we moved outside into the orchard. Barney and Jinny began to dance. Hal pulled me towards the open space under the trees.

'I'm not very good at this,' I protested, laughing. The truth was that Mike had hated modern dancing so I had had very little chance to try it since our marriage.

'What's to be good at?' Hal said. 'Just let yourself go.'

I had never danced like that before, on and on, scarcely conscious of those around me, moving to the rhythm of the music which seemed to have become also the rhythm of the blood in my veins. Hal was close to me, his movements complementary but independent. We were like two birds soaring and turning together in the air. We danced until sheer exhaustion brought us down and we fell side by side under an apple tree.

In the candle-light under the stars Jinny danced on, perfect, self-absorbed. Around her Barney gyrated like a moth about a candle. Under the shadow of a tree Alexis and Paul stood embraced. I had a vague recollection of having seen Tim fast asleep on Old Bill's lap in the kitchen and Simon nodding off on the high-backed settle in front of the range. Hal turned on his elbow and leaned down to kiss me.

Later, at the door of his room, I hesitated, dropping my head against his shoulder.

'Hal, I'm not sure I can. Mike was the only one, you see.'

He took my face between his hands.

'Mike's dead, Nell. And his world's dead too. You can't stay in your safe little nesting box any longer.'

About a week later it was agreed that the show could be tried out in Hay and the first attempt was made to put Bruno into the shafts of the caravan. The April weather had turned as warm as summer and I had borrowed a loose cotton smock from Jinny. I was busy in the kitchen but I could guess from the shouts

211

in the yard that the horse was not taking kindly to the idea.

I could hear the high, excited voices of Simon and Tim as they dodged around the outskirts of the action and occasionally Hal or Barney calling to them to keep out of the way. Then there was a sudden, louder clatter of hooves, a crescendo of shouts, and a silence. It was the silence that brought me to the door.

Hal was crossing the yard carrying Simon in his arms. Simon's head and arms hung limp. Tim came running, screaming 'Mummy! Mummy!' By the caravan Barney and Alexis stood with the horse which was stamping and jerking its head against the halter.

Hal said, 'I'm afraid he got kicked. It's knocked him out. Get some water. He'll be all right.'

We laid him on the settle. There was blood running from his nose and the imprint of the hoof was clearly visible across his cheekbone. He was white and deathly still. I bathed his face, sobbing and calling his name. Paul stood by, holding Tim and trying to reassure him. Hal patted my shoulder and repeated 'He'll be all right,' but when I looked up into his eyes for confirmation he turned his head away. A few moments later Simon was violently sick without regaining consciousness.

When we had cleaned him up I said,

'Hal, he's got to go to hospital.'

'Don't be silly,' he said sharply, 'How can

he?'

'He's got to,' I reiterated. I was not sobbing any longer. Alexis and Barney had come in and were standing by the door.

'How are we going to get him there?' Hal said obstinately.

Paul looked up from comforting Tim and said,

'Lexi . . . ?'

After a second Alexis said,

'There's about a gallon of petrol in the car. Enough to get you to Hereford and perhaps back again. I was keeping it for . . . emergencies.'

'O.K. !' Hal said with sudden violence. 'So you get to Hereford. Then what? They'll want your I.D. cards at the hospital. Then they will want to know where you came from, where you've been living. Next thing, we shall have the KBG out here.'

'Hal!' I cried. 'If I don't take him he could die. He may have a fractured skull or something. I won't tell them where I've been. I'll say we've been squatting in an abandoned farmhouse somewhere else—on our own.'

'Oh yeah?' he said. 'Which one? Tell me the address. How do you get to it?'

Barney put in quickly, 'There's an old farm cottage the other side of the village, by the stream. You know where I mean. If Nell said she'd been there it wouldn't connect her with us.'

213

'And suppose they go and search it?'

'We could go over there and leave some stuff around—blankets, a bit of food, some of their own gear. They wouldn't bother too much about searching. Why should they?'

I looked at him gratefully.

'Thanks, Barney. And you, Alexis. I know it's asking a lot. I've got to go, Hal. I won't mention you, or this place, I promise.'

He hesitated a moment, then nodded.

'O.K. I'll drive you. Is that all right with you, Alexis?'

Alexis handed over the car keys and Hal went out. Barney said,

'It's my fault, Nell. Don't blame the horse. He didn't understand what we were trying to do.'

I swallowed. 'It's not your fault, Barney. I should have kept the boys out of the way.'

The car drew up outside. Rather to my surprise it was Alexis who stepped forward and gently lifted Simon. He moaned slightly but his eyelids did not open. We wrapped him in a blanket and got him onto the back seat of the car. Tim sat by his feet. I got in beside Hal and he let in the clutch. As we bumped through the gate I looked back. They were all standing in a group by the door. I realized that I had not said goodbye.

We drove in silence along the narrow roads between their high hedges. Every now and then I turned in my seat to touch Simon's white face. He stirred once or twice and seemed to be half conscious but he did not speak. At length Hal said,

'What will you do—when he's in the hospital?'

I sat with an empty silence in the pit of my stomach.

'I don't know. It depends how ill he is.'

'You'll stay with him?'

'If they'll let me.'

He said no more.

We entered the outskirts of Hereford. The streets were quiet and there was no sign of damage. It was possible to imagine that the town had escaped the conflicts which had racked the rest of the country. Then two truck loads of soldiers pulled out from a turning in front of us. My stomach turned over. The air of peace was an illusion. The army had moved in here, too. As we drove through the town we saw more army vehicles and twice dispatch riders on motor-cycles passed us. There seemed to be a good deal of activity going on but, to my intense relief, there were no road blocks.

Neither of us had any idea where the hospital was. Hal did not want to stop and ask but eventually I insisted. A kindly woman directed us in a lilting Hereford accent, without apparent curiosity. A few minutes later we drew up outside the casualty department. The first thing we both saw as we did so were two army trucks and a field ambulance pulled up outside. Hal looked at me.

'Looks like there's been some fighting. The whole place is swarming with soldiers.'

'I can't help that,' I said urgently. 'I've got to get Simon to a doctor.'

He shrugged and got out. I helped him lift Simon out of the car. He moaned slightly but his eyes remained shut as Hal carried him into the main reception hall. Thirty or forty soldiers sat around on benches and chairs, most of them with bandages on arms or legs or heads. They were chatting quite cheerfully, indeed there was a certain air of gaiety about the atmosphere. None of them appeared to notice us.

A nurse came forward from behind a desk.

'What happened, dear?'

'He was kicked by a horse,' I said. 'He's been sick. I think it's concussion.'

The nurse beckoned to a porter with a trolley and Hal laid Simon on it. The nurse said,

'I'll get someone to look at him as soon as I can, but, as you can see, we're rather busy at the moment.'

Her tone was matter-of-fact, as if her casualty department was usually full of wounded soldiers.

Hal said, 'I'll just go and shift the car into the car park.'

216

When he had gone I sank down onto a vacant seat and pulled Tim onto my lap. Simon lay still on the trolley. I wanted to shout to someone to come and take care of him but I could only catch glimpses of nurses and doctors as they hurried across the hall.

A soldier sat nearby with a bandage round his head. He was in his middle thirties, I guessed, weathered and tough looking—a professional, I thought. Tucked under the tab on his shoulder was a folded blue beret. I could not recall having seen soldiers in blue berets before.

Tim whispered, 'What's happened to that soldier, Mummy? Has he been shot?'

'I don't know,' I whispered back.

The man had been gazing blankly in front of him. Now he looked round and smiled at us, glad I thought to have something to alleviate the boredom of a long wait.

'Bit of shrapnel, son,' he said. 'Got too near to a shell.'

Shrapnel, shells. I turned the words over in my mind. But who had fired them? Were we in the middle of a civil war, or had we been invaded? In either case, who was fighting whom—and which side of the lines were we on?

'You waiting to see the doctor?' the soldier asked Tim.

'No,' he answered. 'It's my brother.' He indicated with his eyes the stretcher where

217

Simon lay.

The man got up and went over to look at Simon. Then he turned back to me and spoke less casually.

'What happened to him?'

'He was kicked by a horse.'

He bent over Simon for a moment, then said,

'Has the doctor seen him?'

'Not yet. We've got to wait our turn, you see.'

He followed my gaze around the crowded hall.

'We'll see about that. Hang on.'

I watched him cross the hall and speak to an officer, indicating Simon. The officer nodded and beckoned to a nurse and the soldier came back to me.

'His turn next,' he said with a wry grin. 'We're supposed to be in this for the benefit of people like you, not to stop you getting attention when you need it.'

I thanked him rather shakily and he sat down again. It occurred to me that no-one had asked for our identity cards or questioned us in any way. Emboldened I said,

'Can you tell me what is going on, exactly?'

He looked at me with mild curiosity.

'I can't tell you the situation out there,' he jerked his head vaguely eastwards, 'if that's what you mean. That's military information, that is.'

218

'No . . .' I groped for words. 'I don't mean that. I mean, who exactly is fighting whom?'

He looked at me closely.

'Where have you come from?'

'Up in the hills,' I told him. 'I've been—staying—on a farm. It's rather cut off and we didn't have a radio, so I don't know what's been going on.'

'How long have you been there?'

'About a month?'

He nodded slowly as if this explained a good deal.

'Running away from the KBG, were you?'

I swallowed and felt my stomach lurch, but he went on,

'I've come across a lot of people like you lately, hiding up in all sorts of bolt holes away from those bastards. Don't worry. It won't be much longer.'

I stared at him.

'Then you're fighting against the KBG?'

He stared back at me for a moment and then gave a small, explosive laugh.

'Christ! You didn't think I was one of them, did you?' Then, more soberly, 'Well, no reason why you should think any different, I suppose, if you've been out of touch for the last few weeks.'

A nurse came over.

'The doctor will see your little boy now. If you'll just wait here, we'll let you know as soon as the doctor has finished his examination.'

219

Simon was wheeled away. I turned back to the soldier.

'Please, tell me what is happening. Is there a civil war going on?'

He hesitated and fingered the bandage round his head. 'Well, I suppose you could call it that. No . . . well, no, not what you'd call a war. Let's hope it won't come to that. A bit of a skirmish, like.'

'But you are fighting against the government?'

'Against the government as formed by the so-called National Unity Party, yes.'

'And who are you?'

He shrugged and grinned. 'We haven't got a name. People suggested things like The People's Democratic Army and things like that, but we didn't really reckon them. We're just a lot of blokes like me who couldn't stick the way things were going and got out.'

'Out to where?'

'Over the River, into the Forest of Dean. I was serving near Bristol. Soon as I heard General Gray was over there and they'd declared themselves independent I went across the water first chance I got. Lots of others did the same.'

'General Gray?' I repeated.

'Yes. Our Commanding Officer now. Did you come over the River too? You're not from hereabouts, are you? I'm not being nosy. It's just that if you did come that way you probably

220

met him. He always made a point of interviewing refugees himself.'

'Is he a tall, rather thin man, with greying hair?' I asked.

'Yes, that's him. Thought you'd probably run into him.'

I remembered the quietly spoken, courteous man who had helped me to get a lift to Hay.

'I had no idea that he was a soldier.'

'No. He was keeping pretty quiet earlier on—waiting to see how things worked out, I suppose.'

'But now he's leading this—attack?'

'Yep. Got his H.Q. here in Hereford, in the Town Hall—for the time being, anyway.'

'When did all this start?'

'We moved north day before yesterday. They weren't expecting us, of course. Didn't take us long to mop up any resistance. Different kettle of fish today, though. They started moving units north from Gloucester and Oxford as soon as the news got through. We were sent out to hold them off. That's where I got this.'

I frowned at him. Somehow the story still didn't make sense.

'But are there enough of you? I mean, surely you can't take on the rest of the British Army, can you?'

He gave me a long, hard look.

'Listen. I don't know it all, and if I did I couldn't tell you. All I know is that we're not in this alone, I don't know who the others are, or where they are, but when we started out the General told us it wouldn't be more than a few days, and I believe him.'

An orderly called a name. The soldier looked up and rose.

'That's me. Well, all the best. I hope the kid's all right—and don't worry! I'm telling you—in a few days it'll be over.'

He nodded and gave me another wryly humorous grin, then moved away and disappeared down one of the corridors. I realized suddenly that I had seen no sign of Hal. Calling Tim to me I went to the door, and then round the corner of the building to the car park. Alexis's battered old car was quite distinctive, impossible to miss. It was not in the car park. I turned and walked slowly back to the casualty department where I sank down in the same seat as before.

I was roused by a nurse saying,

'Come along, dear. Your little boy's awake now. I expect you'd like to see him.'

I started up. 'Is he all right?'

'We've done an X-ray and the doctor doesn't think there's anything serious. He's with him now. You can talk to him yourself.'

She led us to a little cubicle. It was empty except for the high, white covered table on which Simon looked tiny under the hospital blanket. I went over and looked down at him. His eyes were still closed, I whispered,

'Simon . . . ?'

Slowly the pale lids with their faint tracery of blue veins lifted. His eyes were vague, unfocused, but his lips moved, framing the word, 'Mummy'.

I leaned over and stroked his face and said, very calmly and cheerfully,

'Hello, darling. Don't worry. Everything's all right. You'll soon be feeling better.'

A doctor in a white coat came from the next room.

'Ah, you're his mother? Mrs . . . ? We don't seem to have any particulars yet.'

'Fairing,' I said. 'His name is Simon. Is he going to be all right?'

He came and stood by Simon, looking down at him.

'Yes, I think so. He's had a nasty bang on the head, of course, but the X-ray doesn't show any serious damage. We'll keep him in for a day or two, just to make sure. If you'll just give the nurse some details we'll get him admitted and then you can go up to the ward with him and see him settled.'

The nurse took me to a desk and began to fill in the usual admission form. When I told her our address she looked up and said,

'Oh, you're a long way from home, aren't you?' but she did not pursue the question any further. No one mentioned travel passes or identity cards.

We saw Simon put to bed in a small ward

223

with some other children. He was still very drowsy and very soon drifted off into sleep. A kindly nurse said,

'I should come back this evening, if I were you. He won't know whether you're here or not before then.'

Tim was restless and hungry and I realized that it was well past midday. We went down to the main hall again and bought some sandwiches and a drink at the counter in the corner. As I paid for them I saw that I had hardly any money left. Since we left home I had not dared to go to a bank. While we ate I forced myself once more to consider our situation and make plans.

On the credit side was the fact that we appeared to be, at least temporarily, out of the reach of the KBG. But how long could that last? I had no means of knowing how the battle was going but if General Gray's men were driven back we could soon find ourselves in the middle of it. On the other hand, we had to stay in Hereford until Simon was well enough to leave hospital. Even if I had wanted to get back to the farm it would have been impossible without Hal and the car. But if we were to stay, where could we find accommodation and how was I going to pay for it?

I remembered how General Gray had shaken my hand at the end of our interview in Ross and told me to come back to him if I decided not to go on to Dolgelly after all. Circumstances had changed somewhat since then but I had a feeling that the offer of help had been genuine. I rose to my feet. I had trusted my instinct once or twice before and it had not let me down. I resolved to follow it on this occasion.

At the Town Hall I asked to see the General with a good deal more confidence than I felt, implying a rather closer personal acquaintanceship than I could have justified if challenged. After some consultation by telephone we were shown up to a large, sunny room with a number of desks and tables occupied by half a dozen officers of various ages and ranks. One of them came forward.

'Mrs Fairing? My name is Wilcox. Will you come and sit over here, please.'

He took me to a chair by one of the desks and sat behind it. I was uneasily aware that the other men in the room had stopped whatever they were doing and were listening. I wondered why they should be so interested.

'You say you are a friend of General Gray's?'

'Not a friend, really.' My bravado was beginning to evaporate. 'I met him once in the Forest of Dean. He told me that if ever I needed help I could come to him.'

The face of the young man behind the desk relaxed a little.

'And you need help now?'

225

'Yes—yes, I do.'

'Well, perhaps I can do something. You must appreciate, the General has a great deal on his mind at the moment . . .'

A door opened behind me and there was a sudden scraping of chairs as all the men in the room stood up. I looked round. The man I remembered from Ross stood for a moment in the doorway of an inner office, looking round the room. Then his eyes alighted on me. He took a step forward, frowning with surprise and the effort of recognition. I rose.

'It's Mrs Fairing, isn't it?'

'Yes. General Gray . . . ?'

He gave me his hand and smiled. 'I'm sorry I couldn't identify myself last time we met. But I thought you were on your way to Wales— Dolgelly, wasn't it? What are you doing here?'

I said, 'We never got as far as Dolgelly,' and as I said it I was suddenly aware of an almost overwhelming exhaustion.

He scanned my face for a moment, then, 'Come in here and tell me what happened. Wilcox, bring us some tea, will you?'

He shepherded me into the inner room and seated me in an armchair near the window while he perched on the sill.

'And this is—one of your children?'

'Yes, this is Tim.'

'Hallo, Tim. And how old are you?'

'Eight,' Tim said firmly.

Gray looked back to me.

'I thought . . .' he hesitated, 'I thought you spoke of two boys.'

'Simon's in hospital,' I told him. 'He got kicked by a horse. That's why I'm here.'

'Oh dear!' He looked genuinely concerned. 'I hope it's not serious.'

'He's got concussion, but the doctor says he hasn't fractured his skull or anything. They are keeping him in for observation.'

'How long for? Did they say?'

'A few days.'

He nodded pensively, 'A few days . . .'

The tea arrived. When it was poured out the General said,

'So you never got to Dolgelly. What happened?'

I told him the story, briefly. Even to him I found myself leaving out the exact whereabouts of the farm and the names of the people living there. When I had finished he looked relieved.

'So things haven't been too bad for you.'

I shook my head. 'Not until today. I wouldn't have bothered you with my problems, but I've no money to speak of and without money I can't find anywhere to stay.'

He began to move around the room. I sensed that he was restless and on edge, that I was perhaps a welcome distraction. After a pause he said,

'Tell me, how did you know I was here?'

I related the story of my conversation with

227

the soldier in the hospital.

'You see,' I ended, 'I've no idea, really, what is going on. I—don't want to be here with the children if . . .'

'If we're defeated and the government troops move in.' He finished the sentence for me. He came back to perch again on the window sill. 'I don't think you need to worry about that, Mrs Fairing.'

There was a kind of excitement about him, like someone on the verge of a great event, carefully controlled but unmistakable now.

I said, 'Can you really defeat the NUP?'

He smiled. 'Not us alone. But what if I were to tell you that by tonight we shall have a new government and the whole nightmare will be over?'

I stared at him, shaking my head slightly in disbelief, yet finding myself beginning to smile also.

He gave a short laugh. 'Don't worry. I'm not a Don Quixote tilting at the whole British army—well, what's left of it—with the few men at my disposal. We're only a diversion; one more straw on the NUP's back. Let me explain . . .'

He moved to his desk and sat down, regarding me for a moment in silence. Then he added, more gravely,

'I think you have as much right as anyone to know the truth. In a small way you were instrumental in bringing about the present state of affairs.'

'I was?' I exclaimed,

He nodded. 'You were the first person to bring us reliable information about how weak the government really was. That was invaluable to me in controlling the more—desperate elements in Ross at that time. Also, it was a great encouragement to me personally. Up to that time I had been seriously considering getting out of the country while I had the chance—like so many other people in positions of authority. After talking to you I came to the conclusion that I might be able to play a useful role where I was—and what is happening now is a direct consequence of that decision.'

The General rested his elbows on the arms of his chair, placed his finger tips together and regarded me over them. 'As I said, a number of people have found it—expedient—to go abroad during the last few months; among them members of Parliament from all parties, several senior Civil Servants, and a handful of senior officers from the armed services. To begin with they were scattered all round Europe and in America but after a while I learnt that many of them were collecting in Brussels, the reason being the presence there of Ralph Johnson.'

My brain raced through its limited political Who's Who and, surprisingly, came up with an answer. Ralph Johnson was a moderate, left-of-centre politician who had given up his seat in the Commons to take a post with the Common Market Commission.

The General continued, 'I understand that a move was made to persuade Common Market governments to intervene in the situation over here but, understandably, they were not prepared to interfere with the activities of a government which was, after all, elected by proper democratic processes. However, they did not like the way things were going any more than we did so eventually it was agreed that they would back Ralph Johnson in an attempt to force Emerson to resign, provided that it could be shown that there was massive unrest and dissatisfaction throughout the country.' He paused and added with a wry smile, 'You have to appreciate that the government has kept a very tight control over information leaving the country. Also, the various resistance movements have in many cases been suppressed or have burnt themselves out through lack of food and other supplies. It wasn't that the Europeans did not know how things are here, but they needed a very definite and concrete excuse for their intervention. That's where we come in.'

He rose and moved over to a large map of Southern England which was pinned up on the wall. I think it was a reflex action, produced by so many military briefings.

'I've been in contact with Brussels for some

weeks now. Also, over the last month or two increasing numbers of men have deserted from units in the South West and come to join us. Our biggest stroke of luck was when a complete unit which had been recalled from Northern Ireland diverted to Cardiff and came to join us. They had armoured cars, even a couple of tanks, which have been invaluable. The plan which they concocted in Brussels was this. At dawn yesterday we began a diversionary movement by attacking Hereford, hoping to draw off units which were holding down Oxford, Reading and Bristol. It succeeded very well—almost too well. Our lads are taking quite a pasting down there. However, what matters is that as soon as the units were withdrawn the resistance organizations in those areas staged massive anti-government demonstrations. Brussels was in touch with leaders in a number of areas and there were co-ordinated plans for marches and sit-ins all over the country. Meanwhile, the Scottish Regiments who declared for an independent Scotland at the beginning of all this should have marched over the border to encourage the resistance in places like Newcastle and Liverpool. By now, if everything has gone according to plan, the whole country should be in uproar. At that point the Europeans can step in and force Emerson to resign on the pretext of preventing a civil war. Johnson is standing by at a NATO airfield and as soon as Emerson steps down he will fly over with a number of other leading politicians and form an interim government. By tonight it should all be over.'

I said slowly, 'I can't take it in. It sounds too good to be true.' Then, with sudden embarrassment, 'And here I am bothering you because I've got nowhere to stay!'

He laughed, sounding suddenly youthful and excited again. 'My dear Mrs Fairing, I can't tell you what a relief it has been to talk to you! You see, I've done all I can now, and there's nothing left to do but wait—and waiting can be the hardest part, you know. However,' he moved towards the door, 'we must get you fixed up. We've taken over a couple of hotels, so you've no need to worry. There will be compensation of some sort to be paid, no doubt, when this is all over. Your bill will be covered in that.'

He took me back to the outer office and called Lieutenant Wilcox. As he was giving him instructions to see that we were accommodated a young soldier entered, saluted smartly and handed the General some papers. I felt the stir of excitement that went through the room and understood why my arrival had occasioned such interest. These men, too, had nothing much to do but wait.

The General held out his hand to me. 'Goodbye, Mrs Fairing. I'll keep in touch and let you know when something happens.'

I could see that his mind was really on the contents of the papers and as soon as he had spoken he turned and went back into his room. The little stir of interest which had freshened the room like a breeze died away again.

The Lieutenant said, 'Right, Mrs Fairing. Let's get your hotel fixed up.'

He lifted the telephone but before he could dial the inner door opened again and the General strode back into the room.

'Gentlemen, we've done it! The Government resigned at noon and Ralph Johnson is already in Downing Street!'

Everyone had come to his feet. There was an outcry of triumph and delight. In the babel of orders and congratulations that followed Tim and I were momentarily forgotten. He pressed close to me.

'What's happened, Mummy?'

I hugged him. 'It's going to be all right, Tim. We shan't have to hide any more!'

Miraculously someone produced a bottle of champagne and a moment later a glass was pressed into my hand. I said, laughing with the excitement which had infected me as much as the rest,

'I shouldn't drink your champagne! I've no earthly right to be here at all, especially at this moment.'

No-one would hear of us leaving at that moment, however, and I found myself a guest at an impromptu party which went on for the rest of the afternoon. The General and his officers came and went but the room was never empty and the supply of champagne and fizzy lemonade for Tim was apparently unlimited. Eventually I realized that it was time to go and visit Simon and summoned the will-power to drag myself away, but only after promising the General that I would join him for dinner at the hotel later.

I do not know why I had thought that the rejoicing was confined to that one room. The streets were full of people laughing and shouting. I heard 'Up with Mr Johnson' and 'Long live the Queen' but the most prevalent chant was 'Down with the KBG!' Soldiers of General Gray's force, distinctive in their blue berets, were being embraced and fêted. In one street a huge bonfire was already being built. Nearby stood two crude effigies waiting to be burnt. One was unmistakeably Martin Emerson. The other, I recognized with a jolt, was Jocelyn Wentworth. Where, I wondered, was he now, in reality? And where was Clare?

At the hospital we found Simon wide awake and sporting the beginnings of a spectacular black eye. The nurses and doctors were celebrating, like everyone else, and the festive atmosphere had quite banished any fears Simon might have had about his situation. We stayed for about an hour but when his supper came along I took the opportunity to slip away.

At the hotel I got Tim a light meal and put

him to bed and then went down to join the General and his staff. At the door of the dining room I realized that I was still wearing the loose cotton robe, borrowed from Jinny, which I had been wearing in the kitchen of Brynwcws that morning, in another world. Well, it was all I had, and it seemed oddly fitting that I should finish my journey totally without possessions, not even owning the clothes I stood up in.

I learnt later that for many people that night was a night of long knives, but thoughts like that were far from my mind at the time and if any of the others dining with me guessed at it they did not say so. For that one night, seated beside the General, I was guest of honour at a victory banquet.

Towards the end of the evening he said, 'What will you do now, when your son is well enough to leave hospital? Will you go on to Dolgelly, or will you go home?'

I did not answer at once. The idea that we could now go home if we wished had not occurred to me. At length I said,

'I think I shall go on to Dolgelly, for the time being at any rate. I want to see my parents and let them know we're all right. I suppose we shall go home, sooner or later. Quite honestly, I can't imagine living there under normal circumstances without ...'

He patted my arm. 'Well, you go to Dolgelly and have a good rest. It's what you need. I have to go to London tomorrow but my staff will remain here until everything is sorted out and the men have rejoined their proper units. I'll leave instructions that you're to be given transport. I may be back before you go, but if not just let Wilcox know when you want to travel and he'll arrange it.'

So it was that we eventually arrived at my parents' home in an army Land Rover with a corporal at the wheel. I did not see General Gray again, but I read in the paper some time later that he had been knighted for his services.

Before I left Hereford I wrote to Hal, assuming that the postal service would now return to normal and that eventually the postman would pedal up the long lane to the farm. It was not a long letter; just a few lines to tell him what had happened and what the current situation was—but I suppose Alexis and Paul and Jinny must have found that out when they performed in Hay;—if they ever got Bruno between the shafts of the caravan.

CHAPTER SIX

RECONSTRUCTION

It was mid-summer when we finally returned home. All through the long summer days I had sat in the garden of my parents' home, looking out over the estuary or across to the slopes of Cader Idris. I had been spoilt and pampered and my mother begged me to stay permanently with them, but slowly the realization had grown that I could not start to rebuild my life until we were in our own home again. Cautiously, like a rider with a frightened horse, I brought my brain round to face the barrier of the future.

It was late afternoon when we got out at our little country/suburban station. Like so many of its kind it lay a short distance from the village it was intended to serve, that being the closest point on the line. No-one else got off with us. The evening commuter rush, if it still existed, would not begin for another hour. We walked up the quiet, tree-lined road. The houses here were well set back behind high hedges. There was no way of telling how much they had suffered since we left. We passed the builder's yard. The blackened timbers still stretched, untouched, towards the sky. Next our way lay through a more recent and very expensive development. Here the story became at once clearer, because more visible, and more confused. Some houses were obviously deserted, their windows broken or boarded up, gardens tall with weeds, Others were occupied, but broken panes, littered gardens and collapsing fences made it clear that the occupants had no sense of permanency. Still others maintained defiantly

237

the standards of the original owners, with gleaming paint and vivid flower beds, though even here one could see evidence of the constant struggle to keep out the tide of vandalism and neglect.

We turned into our own road. The boys, who had chattered happily when we first got off the train, clearly delighted to be back, had fallen silent. The houses here were older, more discreet, with tree shaded front gardens, but here the story was the same; some untouched, others neglected and in disrepair; one a burnt out shell. I quickened my step.

We reached the house and stood at the gate, looking at it. The windows were intact; someone had mown the lawn; on the doorstep stood a bottle of milk. My fingers trembled as I fumbled for my latch-key, saying,

'I'm afraid someone may be living in our house.'

'Who?' demanded Simon.

The key turned easily. I let myself in. For an instant the sheer familiarity of the house overwhelmed me. The carpets, the wallpaper, just as I had left them. It even smelt the same! I stood still in the hall, listening. There was no movement. Slowly I went through to the lounge.

In the doorway I stopped with a sudden sick jolt. At first I could not quite make out what was wrong with the room. Then I realized that it had been brutally vandalized but that someone had, as far as possible, repaired the damage. Chair covers had been ripped and then roughly patched or covered. The carpet had been pulled up and tacked down again. Mike's desk had been broken open but had been mended.

It was the same story all over the house. All my clothes had been taken out of cupboards and drawers and pushed back in the wrong places. Some favourite pictures and ornaments had disappeared; books had been ripped. Yet everywhere was evidence that someone had tried to make good the damage and that whoever it was still lived here.

Eventually I called the boys in.

'Someone has spoilt a lot of our things,' I told them, 'but someone else has tried to put it right.'

'Who can it be?' Simon asked.

I shook my head. 'I expect someone who needs a home has moved in here while we've been away. They will probably come back soon, then we shall see.'

Downstairs the front door closed softly. The boys looked up at me without speaking.

'Stay here,' I whispered and went out onto the landing.

Alan stood in the hall. For a moment I almost failed to recognize him. My image of him was still the smooth, well-tailored young executive. Now he was dressed in jeans and carried a greasy boiler suit. He must have lost a stone in weight and his face, once no more than fashionably lean and bronzed, was full of new lines and hollows. He looked up at me and said,

'Nell! Thank God!'

I ran downstairs and threw myself into his arms. The boys clattered after me, shouting,

'It's Uncle Alan! Uncle Alan!'

We clung to each other and he said huskily against my ear,

'I knew you'd come back, sooner or later.'

Then he let me go and turned to tousle the heads of the boys and quiet their questions with,

'Later. I'll tell you all about it later.'

We looked at each other. He said,

'God, you look marvellous!'

I knew that I, too, had lost weight but to advantage, and the last months in the open air had bronzed my skin and bleached highlights in my hair; but the change went deeper than that and I was only now beginning to realize it.

'You look—tired,' I answered.

He gave me a brief flicker of the old, ironic smile.

'Like worn out, you mean. But where have you been? When did you get back?'

I said suddenly, 'Alan, you know about—Mike?'

He reached out and pulled me to him.

'Yes, I heard. Poor Nell.'

'You were fond of him too,' I murmured.

He nodded, still holding me.

'Yes, I was. The stupid thing was I'd known him so long I didn't realize how much. We just took each other for granted, until the last few weeks. That was when I really began to appreciate him—and you.' He paused and I drew back. 'When did it happen?'

'The day you left. You were both here at breakfast and—neither of you came home.'

'Oh my God!' he breathed. 'Oh Nell, if only I'd known!'

'How could you?' I said. Then, 'Come into the kitchen. I'll make some tea or something.'

He gave a sudden laugh.

'You don't know how reassuring it is to hear you say that! You always were the archetypal wife and mother, Nell.'

I paused with my hand on the door, remembering Hal.

'I wouldn't have liked that once, you know. Now I think I'm rather proud of it,'

I made tea and produced the cake my mother had given me. Alan fell on it like manna from heaven. I said,

'What happened to the house?'

'I'm not sure,' he answered. 'When I got back it was in a hell of a state. I suppose it was vandals, but it looked just as though they had been searching for something. Everything was ripped open, turned upside down, God knows what they were looking for.'

Light dawned then. 'I think I know,' I said.

241

'And who it was. Have you seen or heard anything of that man Harrington?'

Alan looked slightly surprised. 'Funny you should ask that. He was killed just a week or two ago. His house caught fire. Apparently he was trapped in an upstairs room.'

I put the tea on the table and sat down. Alan reached for my hand.

'Now tell me everything. Where have you been?'

'With my parents in Dolgelly.'

'Of course,' he cried. 'I guessed you might be but I didn't know their address and I couldn't find a single letter or anything. No wonder you look so well. You've been out of it all up there.'

I put my head in my hands and began to laugh weakly. 'What have I said?' he asked.

I told him the story of what had happened after he left and my journey. The boys had drifted off to rediscover old toys so I told him the whole thing frankly, including Hal.

When I finished I found he was looking at me intently.

'Nell, you amaze me,' he said. 'Talk about sheer guts and dogged determination! I really admire you for not giving up against those odds.'

I shook my head. 'It was just a question of not having any alternative. Perhaps that's what most courage is. Anyway, tell me about you.'

He sighed. 'Not a very creditable story, I'm

242

afraid. When I left here I headed west, like you, but south-west in my case. I knew it was no good heading for the Midlands with so much unemployment there already. I thought perhaps I could find something in a smallish country town. I tried Winchester and Salisbury and all the villages round. There was nothing. I picked up a bit of casual work, here and there, mostly labouring. Otherwise I lived on the dole. That isn't easy, by the way, when you've no roof over your head. Then the election came and the emergency regulations and next time I went to draw my money I was told I couldn't have it but I could have a job, in the docks at Bristol. I was put on a coach with a load of other fellows and we were driven to an old army barracks which had been turned into what they called a 'hostel'. It turned out to be a sort of labour camp! We didn't know what was going on, of course, but we soon found out. The dockers had gone on strike and were refusing to go back, in spite of the regulations. There was no Social Security money for their families and the union's assets had been frozen so there was no strike pay, either. There was hardly any food in the shops. The only way to get it was on the Black Market, and that soon used up any savings they had. They were literally starving. Every morning we were marched down to the docks under armed guard. They said it was for our own protection! Well, if it hadn't been there I daresay none of

243

us would have reached the dock gates. We'd either have joined the strikers voluntarily or been lynched! They used to come out every morning and stand in the streets in twos and threes, so as not to break the law against public meetings, not saying anything, just looking at us. There was one chap I'll never forget as long as I live. He used to come to a particular street corner with his whole family—very pregnant wife and two little girls. They just used to stand there and every day they got thinner and paler. The kids had huge shadows under their eyes and the wife was just a skeleton with a huge stomach—obscene! Then one day she wasn't there. Just as we got to him he started to shout. 'You've killed her, you bastards! Blackleg bastards!' Two of the guards pounced on him and marched him away. The last I saw the little girls were running after them shouting, "Let go of my daddy!"'

He broke off and put his hand over his eyes. I reached out and took the other.

'Was there no way of getting away from it?'

He shook his head.

'We were literally imprisoned in that "hostel". We were told that if we went out we would be mobbed, which was probably true, The place was guarded day and night. We were planning to escape, of course. It was like one of those old POW movies. But in the end the government fell before we could get anything organized.'

'And then?'

'Well, I found myself free but still out of a job and with no home to go to. I decided to come back and see how you and Mike were making out. Of course when I got here the place was empty. The next door neighbour told me about Mike. I hope you didn't mind me moving in.'

'Good heavens no!' I met his eyes. 'I'm so thankful you're here—really.'

He squeezed my hand. I went on,

'But you're working now?'

'Yes!' There was a sudden warmth in his face. 'You remember that little light engineering works out on the main road— Myntori's Metal Products?'

'Yes.'

'Well, it was a father and son concern. The old man died a few months back and the son found he couldn't cope on his own. He's O.K. at the mechanics but he can't manage the costing and marketing side, particularly under present conditions. I went in there one day, just on the off chance. He was thankful to get someone in who knew the business end. It's not a big enough concern to support someone just doing the white collar work; we both have to muck in. But he's taken me into partnership, and things are looking up already. We're making useful things, things that everyone needs but which are in short supply

245

at the moment—ladders, farm equipment, shelves and brackets, that sort of thing.' He smiled at me. 'It's never going to be an international giant, but it's a living.'

'Oh Alan, that's wonderful,' I whispered. 'That's the best thing I've heard for weeks!'

We were quiet for a while until it occurred to me to ask,

'Have you heard anything from Clare?'

He sat looking into his empty cup.

'Not directly, but there was a piece in one of the papers. They were agitating for Emerson and his crew to be tried as traitors or something. Apparently no-one knows where Emerson is—they think South America somewhere—but there was a photograph of Jocelyn Wentworth in Rhodesia. Clare was with him. I don't suppose she'll be back.'

'I'm sorry,' I said quietly.

'You needn't be.' He looked up at me. 'My marriage to Clare was the most stultifying experience in my life. I wouldn't want to have her back now, particularly,' he grimaced and grinned faintly, 'slightly shop-soiled from Jocelyn Wentworth.'

We smiled at each other. He said,

'By the way, have you heard from Jane?'

'No. I wrote to her but she didn't reply. I'm a bit worried about her.'

'You needn't be. She's not at Well Cottage any more because she's living with a man she met during the trouble, over the other side of

Guildford. She phoned a few weeks back, wanting you. I didn't know about her having been in prison, of course. I thought she was a bit cryptic on the phone. Anyway, I told her I thought you were in Wales but I didn't know the address. She left a number for you to call.'

'I'll ring her later,' I said, 'or tomorrow, perhaps. Thank goodness she's all right. Are the children with her? Did she say?'

'Yes. She said particularly to tell you the children were there. I couldn't understand why at the time.'

'I wonder who it is she's living with,' I mused. 'Probably no-one I know. She didn't tell me her contacts. I'm glad she's found someone.'

Later that evening when the boys were in bed we sat together in the lounge. We had talked almost non-stop through supper and now we had fallen silent, but neither of us felt inclined to turn on the radio or the television. At length Alan said,

'You know, Nell, I can't get over you. I'd always thought of you as the quiet little home-body—not the strong, independent type at all. You seem to have discovered a completely new personality.'

I thought about this quietly for a moment.

'I don't think I have, Alan. I've discovered the sort of person I really am—but it's the person I've always been. I used to feel very inadequate compared with Clare and Jane,

247

you know. They seemed to lead such "full" lives. I felt it was very dull and unenterprising of me just to want to stay at home and look after Mike and the kids. I used to pretend that I'd never had the opportunity to really discover my full potential. Well, I've had it now, and I've learned not to undervalue myself. And I've also learned that there is only one kind of life I really want. I've had excitement and adventure, and I've tried the hippy way of life where you don't have to do anything unless you want to and I think I've learned something from that too. But it's not for me, Alan. I did it in order to keep the children and I'd do it all again if I had to, but only for that reason. All I want now is a quiet, ordered life, with no worries except the ordinary, everyday ones.'

He said, 'I think you should be able to have that. It's not going to be like the old days, of course. Not for a long time, anyway. No luxuries, no holidays abroad, not much entertaining or going out. No car and no new kitchen gadgets. But enough to eat and a roof over our heads, and education for the children. You can be pretty sure about those.'

'It's all I want,' I replied.

After a moment he said hesitantly,

'Nell, I've been sort of assuming I can stay here. Of course, you may not want me. You may feel it wouldn't be right, under the circumstances.'

I smiled at him. 'I honestly don't think that sort of "what will the neighbours think" morality matters any more, Alan—not to me at any rate. Of course I want you to stay.'

He rose and came to sit on the arm of my chair.

'I can't tell you how grateful I am to hear that, Nell. I've never been so lonely in my life as I have these last few months.'

I leaned my head against his arm.

'Me, too.'

'I'll take care of you and the boys, of course.' He stroked my hair softly. 'That goes without saying.'

I found myself thinking of a line of Shakespeare. Where was it from? Something about 'down on your knees and thank heaven, fasting, for a good man's love'.

Later, going up to bed, he hesitated outside the door of the room he used to share with Clare. We looked at each other. I said,

'You might as well move into my room—don't you think?'

Sometime during the night he began to talk about divorcing Clare so that we could get married. I told him that it wasn't necessary, but later, on the edge of sleep, I murmured,

'If we ever do get married, I know a smashing vicar called Philip Woodstock. Do you think we could have a honeymoon in South Wales? There are lots of people I'd like to visit.'

249

'One day,' he promised. 'One day.'

In the morning I woke to a familiar but long unheard sound. Outside in the early sun the bin men were clattering rubbish into the council dustcart.